THE BOY WHO FELL FROM THE PAST

OTHER WORKS BY TRUANT MEMPHIS

Littlethumb Sneezed
Post Oh!pocalypto Poppycock
Daffodil

THE BOY WHO FELL FROM THE PAST

<u>*An Introductory Novella*</u>

Truant D. Memphis

Preface

This adventure was first transcribed by my godmother, Pooter, in the early to mid-1990's of my true timeline (I think…), while I was out chasing my windmills. For what it's worth, I'm not typically the sort who refers to oneself in the third person.

t.m.

I

Truant crashes into the water and sinks like a rock. After he gathers his bearings and swallows a mouthful of the nastiest, filthiest water he's ever tasted, he struggles for the surface as tiny objects whizz by. Unprepared for plunging into water, his lungs scream for oxygen while he swims toward the surface with all the strength he can muster. Before reaching the surface, he feels a sharp pain in the back of his left leg. He stops swimming and grabs at his calf muscle. Everything goes black.

Our traveler wakes on his back, head propped, choking, and for some reason his left leg throbs like mad. After several minutes he remembers what happened. At least, he remembers that of which he's aware. The portal.

I landed in water, he thinks. Eyes creak open on a man and a boy. The man guides a rudder. The boy looms over Truant, hair blowing in the wind. It's a small boat, unlike any Truant's seen and moving fast. The materials are patchworked together, forming a hull with a deep well in the center. The boy appears concerned and Truant quickly realizes he'd almost drowned.

"I wasn't sure you were going to make it."

An attempt to reply instead chokes more of the dirty water from Truant. The taste turns his stomach. Searching for the edge of the boat, he leans over the side and vomits. When he's finished, he sinks back down and notices the blood leaving his leg.

"Yeah, lie still. I'll fix it for you. You weren't breathing. Had to get the water out of you first. Don't worry, it looks like a lot of blood but it's not that bad." The boy goes to work cleaning and bandaging the injured leg. When he pokes a gooey resin down into the hole, Truant passes out once more.

When Truant wakes again the boat idles, gently rocking back and forth. The man and the boy sit in front of him eating. Intently watching.

"What happened?"

"I should ask you the same thing." The man's voice is deep, mercury flowing over gravel.

"Sir, I don't think you would believe me if I told you, but…" His words are broken by a coughing fit and the boy hands him a canteen.

"You shouldn't talk too much." The boy speaks with food in his mouth and before he can say anything else the man quietly corrects him.

"Thank you for helping me."

Gulping down his rations to appease his father, the young fella says, "I think you swallowed a lot of that water. It's not good for you. You're probably going to get a real bad stomach ache."

Instinctively looking at his belly, Truant realizes he's wearing more clothes than when he went through the portal. He pulls at a sleeve, inspecting it, then realizes his neck is wrapped and there's weight on his head. A hat. Who's hat?

"My boy is a young man who travels with many hats and a grown man's noggin. We pulled some clothes from your bag. You must stay covered in the sun. It's not good for you."

Self-inspection complete, Truant turns eye to his rescuers. The boy is blond with long unruly hair. His face glows with childish chub.

Behind the cheeky puff lies a strong resemblance to the man and, despite his father's quip, what looks to be a fairly normal-sized head, though apparently large enough for one of his hats to fit Truant.

The man is bulky, a bit taller than Truant and handsome but haggard, with eyes like creeping time that speak to the burdensome weariness of long suffered pain. His hair is much darker than the boy's, but their resemblance is still strong.

Further review of his rescuers exposes a style choice that frightens Truant. Guns. One under the man's arm and two at his hips. Truant does not like guns. He returns his attention to the boy, who follows Truant's eyes intently. The kid is armed as well.

"Don't worry," says the boy. "We should be safe now."

"Where are we?"

"Michigan. Maybe Ohio. Somewhere about two hours south of Detroit City."

"Detroit? Are we on…which one is it…Lake Erie? I don't understand." There's nothing but water in all directions, as if they're adrift upon an ocean.

"These are the northern waters. We won't make solid land until much further south."

Confusion blankets Truant's face.

"My name's Jacob Trate, and that's my dad, Ezekiel."

Truant looks to the man, who nods hello.

"You may call me Zeke."

"And you can call me Jake. I like it better. What's your name?"

"Truant. Truant Memphis."

"Memphis?" Jake responds with a smile. "That's a city."

"Yes it is."

"Are you from there?"

"Never even been to Tennessee that I know of."

"You fell out of the sky. I didn't see anything and then you just crashed into the water. Where did you come from?"

"Would it be okay if we get to that in a minute? I'm a little foggy. I promise I'll try to explain, but…it might take me a little while to figure out how to say it." His eyes move from Jake to Ezekiel. "Is it okay if I ask a couple of questions?"

"Your eyes question the firearms." There's a brief softness in Zeke's expression. "Where are you from young man, that you are surprised to see weapons in the outer rim?"

"I'm from Texas. What's an outer rim?"

"You're clearly out of place. I figure you will explain that in fair exchange." This feels more like an order from Zeke than a suggestion.

Suddenly adverse to eye contact, Truant resurveys his injured leg.

"You were shot, but the bullet passed through safely. A surface wound. My son and I…well, for the time being you're safe with us."

"I was shot?" (He can't *not* look up again on those words, right?) "Who shot me? Why?"

"They were shooting at us. Now, this may seem unfair but before I discuss our situation further, a little information on your part." Zeke casually taps the hammer of the gun on his right hip, outside of Jake's view.

"One more question please, if I may?"

Zeke nods agreement.

"What's today's date?"

"July the 12."

"What year?"

"3023. What year would you have it be?" Zeke's expression betrays a man who might be feeling jerked around.

"Sir, like I said before, I'm afraid it will be hard for you to believe what I have to say." If Truant's voice lacks any sincerity, his face certainly does not.

"You should try telling first, and then we will see."

Jake sits quietly, an intense expression of curiosity on his face. There are moments he appears to have something to add but he keeps his lip tight. Truant turns to him, as if looking at the young fellow will help ease the words from his mouth. Truant is, after all, still closer to being a boy than a man.

"Sir, I think I've traveled through time." Truant speaks with as much nerve as he can muster for words he knows any reasonable human would assume are complete bull schnitzel.

"Whoa!" Jake can't contain himself. Ezekiel maintains a stoic calm, perhaps muddled with quiet disbelief.

"You think you've traveled through time?"

"Well, sir…"

"You may call me Zeke."

"Well, Zeke, I can't think of a good reason why you would lie to me about what year it is, so if it's really 3023, then I have traveled through time, because I was born in 1976, and I've only recently turned seventeen years old."

"It is indeed 3023. I suppose you understand, I might wonder if you're lying?"

"Dad, he fell out of the sky!"

"Jake."

Jake closes his mouth promptly, but Zeke puts a soft hand on his shoulder. The gesture makes Truant more comfortable.

"My son has a point," Zeke says, giving Jake's shoulder a squeeze. "If I should believe what you say, you must explain yourself further. Most importantly, the fact that you appeared as if from thin air."

"Well, I suppose I did. I came through a portal. I jumped into it somewhere far from here, in my time, and the next thing I knew I crashed into the water."

"A portal?"

"It's a long story to tell if I'm going to ask you to believe me, but I will tell you. I can only assume I'm here with you for a reason. Hopefully when I'm finished explaining you'll agree."

"We've got a long way to travel yet. Plenty of time to listen." Zeke's eyes shift cautiously. "Speaking of which, we should get moving. It's not safe to sit still for long outside of the cities, and it will be night soon. Would be nice to find some form of landing before dark." Quietly idling the boat forward, Zeke nods at Truant. "I'll keep the engine low and quiet. Tell your story, Truant Memphis. I'll reserve my judgment until you are finished, as best I can."

"Okay. Uhm, I guess I'll go back to the beginning." The beginning is a quick summation of losing his parents, "My parents died when I was young," followed by his time at the orphanage, "and I lived at an orphanage ran by my godmother until I was sixteen," and eventually leaving Texas for adventure, "then I left Texas to go on an adventure."

Truant's early travels receive the fast-forward treatment until the discovery of an old service station and an elderly black man named Curtis Gout. The story slows and grows more detailed about his months spent training with Curtis, and the portal. Throughout the story, Truant intermittently falls silent with wonder at the water surrounding them. They are, in fact, in northern Ohio, still traveling over deep water.

"So, Curtis gave me his brother's magic watch." As he speaks, Truant pulls a small plastic box from his backpack. Once clear, the plastic case is presently covered in stickers. Truant opens it and removes the timepiece given to him by Curtis Gout. "I know magic sounds crazy but this watch is connected to the portal somehow, that's for sure. I guess it could be science. Technology. Not magic. But, anyway, after all the time I spent at the filling station, me and Curtis both knew what I was supposed to do. So I jumped into the portal. I don't think I would have found that filling station if I wasn't supposed to. Honestly, as crazy as it sounds, I kind of think the filling station found me."

Silence takes over. Truant marvels at Jake's ability to bite back his questions when clearly excited by Truant's tale. The boy's self-control holds Truant's tongue as well, but eventually he can no longer take the quiet.

"What do you guys think?"

Jake opens his mouth for excited words to burst forth but at the last moment holds back, deferring to his father.

"I think you tell your story true."

South through future Ohio in the small boat. Uncertain if it's his future or some alternate dimension, Truant passes most of the day chatting with Jake, looking for clues. He's so entrenched in the conversation he doesn't waste much wonder on whether he'll make it back to his own time or place. (Honestly, I may not have cared. I'm not certain. Can't remember...)

Jake explains the flooding, brought on by climate change hundreds of years before he was born.

"Well at least Canada got what they deserved," Truant jokes, unintentionally launching a discussion about the contentious relationship between Canada and the former United States during their years of preparation for the flooding.

Speaking of which, Jake, with help from Zeke, explains the downfall of the United States government and subsequent dismantling of the U.S. as a nation. Disastrous efforts financing the country. Dereg-ulated, unfettered capitalism. Endless imperialistic efforts overseas. Completely ineffective and unbalanced taxation. Yadda, yadda, fill in the blank here. You're most likely living through it right now un-less you're living after it happened. One way or the other, in the year 2748 the United States found itself effectively bankrupt, though still careening forward as an institution. Without federal funding, many states began selling shares of cities into public ownership. Congress loved the idea and taxed the sales to support their ridiculous salaries. The Great Sell-Off, as it was known, began with modestly sized towns but only got bigger and better. The American way.

In 2814, almost fifty years after most of the major cities in the United States had been sold, a young, successful financier pur-chased majority ownership in the city of New York. He was rebellious and handsome and charismatic. His name was Jon Smith. Jon Smith was secretly a Native American. His voters just thought he had a great tan.

After purchasing New York, Jon Smith ran for President on a platform devoted to the common man and cleaning up govern-ment. Clean it up he did. Shortly after taking office, he locked the doors to Congress, opened up the sale of American cities to in-ternational investors (illegal until this point), and formed the League of Cities.

The League of Cities, still active, was originally an open vote democracy for all citizens. A coup was attempted by members of the old Congress to fight John Smith's deconstruction, but the rest of the world brought the threat of war in a combined effort never before seen, and with many of its own largest cities set against it, the U.S. Government officially crumpled. Congress, along with all federal institutions, was disbanded. States were given back their sovereignty and left to negotiate with the private and corporate owned cities. With no federal government left to preside over, John Smith disappeared. I like to think he eventually got what he deserved, whatever that may be (you decide…). One way or the other, his pail carried no water for what the League of Cities became. The corruption of the League of Cities was simply the course of human dickery-doo.

Along with other cities in the flood zones, Detroit had grown out of the water into three levels: The high city where the wealthy lived, the surface level, and everything under the water. Only the wealthy, high-level dwellers were free citizens. The surface level and the dwellings below the water were filled with property citizens, owned by the Detroit Commonwealth, which was in turn owned by the notorious Primm family. Citizens of the lower levels were not allowed to leave the city or to enter the upper level without permits. Unfortunately, over the years following John Smith's disappearance, the working class had once again slowly eroded their own rights in exchange for short-term gains, eventually finding themselves completely under the thumb of an ownership class yet again. They are confined to a dismal life under the shadow of the gold-plated metropolis above and terrorized by a police force that is nothing more than a licensed crime syndicate. Detroit's borders extended in a large radius circling the city called the outer rim, a lawless area of desperate survival.

"So you shot your way out of the city?"

"Yep, dad was a gunfighter in the upper levels. The best there ever was."

"A gunfighter? Like from the old west."

"If I am not mistaken," says Zeke. "It is not quite the same. It's sport in the upper levels of Detroit. Other cities as well. They take poor men and watch them kill each other. Watching the poor kill each other for sport has been practiced many times and many ways in history. It's a disgrace, though I admit, as a younger man I didn't think of things that way." Remorse creases Zeke's forehead. Eyes pinched by shame-ridden crow's feet stare a thousand miles down a road lined with dead bodies.

"Were you really the best?" Truant is impressed, sort of. Definitely impressed, just not sure if he should be.

"I'm alive. And I was touted a champion, but in the end that meant very little. I lived on the water with the rest of the poor, and my son was destined for the same life. I will not have it. Jake will be free."

The Trate's plan, as it turns, is to make their way to Antarctica, the last free territory left on the Earth. Truant doesn't know what else to do at this point, so he sets his mind on tagging along.

Clear skies grace the travelers' floating camp that evening, though not much sleep is had. Truant and Jake whisper through their first watch while Zeke snoozes with one eye open. Apparently, Jake's mother was from a wealthy, upper-level family. Infatuation with Zeke led her into the lower levels.

Infatuation quickly turned to love, a love celebrated passionately and secretly for many months. Her name was Catherine. When Catherine became pregnant, she refused to name the father and was summarily disowned by her own aristocratic papa. A friend sheltered her and Zeke in the upper levels while she carried Jake to term. All children in the lower levels were marked with serial numbers at birth, property of the City. Jake escaped this branding at desperate peril. Catherine died in labor, the cost of attempting the birth in secret. Zeke fled back to the water, keeping Jake hidden from the city for ten years. It was, however, the discovery of the unregistered youth that had forced Zeke's hand and led to their escape.

At his bladder's urgings, Truant wakes in the middle of the night. Initially resistant to his body's call for adjustment, he sits quietly. Jake snores. Zeke, on watch duty, journals by moonlight.

"Zeke, do you mind if I ask what you are writing?"

"No I do not."

Zeke continues to write in silence. Truant relieves himself over the side of the boat. After sitting back down with no further response from Zeke, Truant gets the joke.

"Zeke, what are you writing?"

Zeke looks at Truant with a quick smile and says, "I'm writing a history, of myself and my son, and of the world as I have seen it until now."

"That sounds like a lot of work."

"I'm hopeful to have plenty of time." Zeke studies Truant's face and relents to more explanation. The boy is out of place and curious. Of course he wants to talk. "When we reach our destination, I cannot assume books will be available for Jake to learn from. And I want to make sure people know the things I've seen and read, just as I hope to learn from others. So, I'm writing a history for our new life, especially for Jake to have if we don't make free land together."

"Do you think I could read it sometime? I've been keeping a journal too, since I left home. Maybe we can swap, share our stories."

"Perhaps."

That look on Zeke's face. Right or wrong, Truant interprets it as, *Probably thinks I'm a runaway rich kid or something.*

"Here is something I will tell you about growing up where Jake and I are from. The schools in the lower levels do not teach history. They do not teach you about cultures. They do not teach you to read. They test your natural physical and mental abilities and then assign you to workstations. That's what you learn as a child. Your work."

"How did you become a gunfighter? Is that a job they gave you?"

"No. I volunteered. I was angry."

"Oh. So, where did you learn to read and write?"

"Jake's mother."

"Well, it's awesome what you're doing. Writing everything down."

"What's awesome mean?" Jake stirs, wearing a puppy's sleepy face.

"People don't say awesome anymore? Weird. I would have bet on that one sticking around. It's like fantastic or great, but even better I guess."

"Oh, like flipped. We say flipped. Well, dad doesn't." Jake smiles. "When we escaped Detroit today, that was awesome."

"There you go. You can keep that one for free, but the rest are gonna cost you. Now you can hang out with comic book nerds, board game geeks, skaters, anybody."

"Awesome?" Jake's quick. He isn't sure if he is being teased, but he is certainly suspicious.

"Zeke, I got another question."

"Ask, and if I don't want to answer, I won't." His tone is more inviting than his words might be perceived here on paper.

"What's it like to, you know, I don't know how the best way to ask."

"Just ask."

"What's it like to shoot someone?"

Jake's mouth falls open.

"Bold," says Zeke.

"I'm sorry. I don't mean to offend. It's just, well, for all I know I could wake up on the moon tomorrow. My life's been kinda crazy that way lately. I don't know how much time we'll have together, and you're the first person I've ever met that I know of who's…you know. I'm sorry. Never mind. That was rude. I'm being rude."

"Do they have Bibles where you come from, Truant?"

Surprise!

"Yeah, they do."

"Well they don't where I am from. Not for the poor. The books I have read, the histories I have learned, were afforded me by the gun. It's paradox. Killing allowed me to read books that taught me killing is wrong. I read philosophies. Logics. Poetries. Books about war. Books about peace. Religion books, like the Bible, which have plenty of war, but also very clear messages of peace."

"Do you believe in a god?" Truant found religion curious, but not curious enough to risk getting involved.

"Gods don't concern me. What I believe is that before I learned to read, shooting another man was a means to an end. A skill. A skill I had a great ability for, and I took glory in my ability. When you ask what it is like to shoot another man, my answer is it depends on what you've learned. I know now it is wrong. To others that may seem obvious. It's not so obvious when people are cheering."

"I guess not."

"But, I learned. If I don't value the life of others, in the end, they have no reason to truly value mine. It's logic." Zeke pauses, his face a clay of fond remembrance and regret twisted around each other. "I don't want Jake to wear a gun. I don't want him growing up in a place where a man finds glory by shooting other men. To do the things that I've done." Any fond remembrance drains from Zeke's face, leaving nothing but pale regret.

Truant allows the man enough quiet for the regret to fade as well, then says, "Zeke, thanks for pulling me out of the water."

"You are welcome. Now, I know it may not be easy, but it is late and tomorrow is another long day. You should try to sleep." Zeke nods at Jake who has already dozed back off. "He'll be running circles around you in the morning."

Hypnagogia. The curse of the waking dream. A scourge upon restfulness. An unyielding tapestry of a thousand maybes, a thousand what-ifs. A thousand lives lived with any potential significance to any particular vision a Jungian needle in an Edgar Cayce haystack. Our boy watches the scenes unfold, emotions racing. Some are sad, some are fantastic, some are too ridiculous to ever come true, and all the while the same refrain: The journey is you, the journey is you.

Shortly before dawn, Truant wakes again. Not his bladder this time. Noises. Visceral instinct commands a silent transition from sleeping to waking world. Jake rustles briefly then grows quiet again. Zeke's left eye peeks open. A pistol slides into his lap.

Truant doesn't want to see the gun at work. He has no interest in firearm fun or gun-toting glory or smoking steel sex appeal, or any other childish notions of heroic death-dealing. In the quiet, he searches for the sign, the uncommon noise that will tell him the truth. Or no sound at all, also very honest though requiring more patience.

There it is. Something touches the side of the boat. Sound and color, tinny and frightening. To the right, the other side of the boat, closer to Zeke.

A hand appears on the edge of the bow. Truant watches Zeke's eyes. Another hand on the bow and the tension grips Truant's throat, cutting his breath. The top of a head shows, rising slowly in silence.

Zeke's movement is swift. Effortless. A goggled mask appears over the bow, greeted by the barrel of Zeke's pistol. The creature lowers itself back into the water as slowly and quietly as it had risen. Truant assumes it was a man but isn't certain.

Zeke looks at Truant and winks, then holds his finger over his mouth telling Truant to remain quiet. He draws another pistol and shouts into the oncoming morn. "I got more 'en one in here and they're all fast. You'll be shot. I promise."

"Relax. We thought it was a floater. Didn't know you were in there. You can put those things away. We'll be moving along." The voice is yards from the boat and irritated. Who or whatever the voice came from continues to mutter petty invectives until out of earshot. Despite the promise of peace, Zeke waits several minutes before holstering his firearms. Then he begins to giggle, and Truant gladly joins him.

The boat creeps through morning fog as Truant escapes his third bout with restless slumber. Jake is still asleep. Zeke stares down the rising sun, enjoying a smoke.

"May I have one of those?"

Zeke lights a roll and tosses it to Truant. "Coffee in that tin there, if you like."

Truant lips the smoke and pours a cup, wondering how the can was heated, but he's too wrapped in morning dumb to give much thought to anything, so he sits with his coffee and his tobacco and allows his mind to wander back and forth from nowhere.

Eventually, the overnight proceedings boil in his brain stew. "Who do you think it was last night, trying to get in the boat?"

"Scavengers. No one dangerous, this time. We're likely to see more, and most won't be so easy to back off. I sat a while last night, expecting them to come back in force. Boat not worth the fight, I suppose."

Jake rousts wide awake and silently dives into making breakfast. A small, flameless burner explains the hot coffee. With limited means, Jake quickly proves himself a worthy galley chef.

"Jake, this is fantastic. And on a boat. You're gonna have to teach me a thing or two."

"It's easy when you're hungry. I could eat my own fingers in the morning." Miming a giant bite into his left-hand digits, Jake begins to laugh with an open mouth, spraying food about and taking Truant along for the ride. Zeke joins in, though his chuckles are nothing like the surprising fit of giggles Truant witnessed the night before. Intently studying his new compatriots, Truant doesn't notice the other boats forming a perimeter around them. They're at a good distance on all sides, attempting obscurity but working in pattern. Herding.

After breakfast, Truant turns his focus to the surrounding waters. In his pain and confusion the day before, he didn't fully absorb the City of Detroit as they sped away from the looming metropolis. Now he soaks in the view of his country covered in water as Zeke guides the boat into what had once been a factory town. The top floors of buildings rise out of the water, along with a series of smokestacks to the east. The water is much clearer now than the day before, exposing the buildings below the surface. "What happened to the people that lived out here, and farmers, and people who lived in small towns?"

"Most people moved to big cities," Jake says, "but some of them stayed. There's still people that live out here. And down there."

"Below the water?"

"Oh yeah. There's whole towns down there. The water came slow and people got ready for it. Buildings were fixed so people could live in them after they went underwater. They grow food down there and everything. Me and Dad lived underwater in an old restaurant underneath Detroit."

"Man, I like the water, but living in it?"

"The restaurant was awesome. There was an elevator inside I used to get to my bedroom. Dad called it my knucklehead chute. And we had a secret basement."

"I'm sorry, I didn't mean you guys. That does sound pretty cool. I was thinking of out here. Living underwater in the middle of nowhere. I just don't understand why people didn't leave."

"People didn't want to leave their homes," Zeke says, "their communities. Some people are born to follow the wind, some grow roots."

"Yeah, that was a silly question, I guess, but why not build above the water? Surface level. Floating cities. Rooftop gardens. That type of stuff."

"They did, but as Jake said, the waters came slow. The first efforts were made shoring up the existing structures. People didn't want to believe how bad it would be. Scientists projected how far underwater different areas would become, but it happened so gradually people resisted. The government, this was before the collapse when we were still the United States, the government tried to get everyone to move, either to the cities or somewhere closer to the middle of the country where they assumed dry land would remain, but most people wouldn't leave. Eventually, the government gave up and helped the communities prepare for the flooding. It was all futile, but it was what the people wanted."

"So where is everybody? All these buildings, it seems like this would be a perfect spot for there to be a city."

"Just because you can't see it, doesn't mean it isn't there."

Another long, slow scan of his surroundings coupled with thoughts of his present circumstances boating through a future covered in water, and Zeke's words take on deeper meaning.

"I guess not," Truant eventually responds.

"When the government fell, there were scarce laws outside the big cities. No more peace-keeping patrols. And the flooding continued. Waters got deeper. Now, those who remain have to be careful. It's dangerous out here."

"You trying to scare me, Zeke?"

The tone is playful, the question largely earnest. Zeke surprises with a touch of charming caution.

"Maybe a little."

"Geez…"

Laughs all around, and a coffee refill. They pass through the heart of the city's remnants before the chat continues.

"How long ago was it, when everything was flooded like this?"

"Over five hundred years!" says Jake.

"How do you know so much if you didn't go to school?"

Perceptive as he is, Jake doesn't register the facetious tone in Truant's question and points to his father with pride. The answer, of course, is what Truant assumed, though Jake's finger-point triggers standard suggestive reactionary brain function, sending Truant's eyes in Zeke's direction, only to notice Zeke's peepers darting about like an ion with attention deficit disorder in an electrical storm.

"Okay, so, these floods were five hundred years ago or so. And at first people made their cities capable of existing underwater. Then built on top of the water too. But the water kept rising, and things got even more dangerous so the people had to hide more, and stopped living on the surface as much."

"Correct."

"And we think people still live in some of the communities underwater?"

"I'm certain, though it's impossible to know how many. Or what those communities have turned into." There's a tension in Zeke's voice that has nothing to do with their conversation.

On cue, Truant catches a glimpse of movement in the window of a large old factory. Three stories of the building are above water. The structure is made of dingy yellow brick and faced with rows of large windows all the way across, all of which are empty of glass.

Brains play tricks, Truant knows. Uncertain if he'd truly seen the thing in the window, there is no question he sees a small craft darting in between the two old smoke stacks of another building. He sits facing Jake, wondering if Jake saw it too, if the boy is afraid. *I don't know why you're worried about him,* Truant thinks. *He's a futuristic mini gunfighter. I'm sure he's less frightened than you.*

To the left more factories climb out of the water. Our runaways are in the heart of an old industrial complex. Row after row of yellow brick and Truant is feeling boxed in. Claustrophobia must show on his face 'cause Zeke takes notice.

"I'll get us out of here as quick as possible. There is plenty of cover. It works just as well for us as them."

"Who do you think they are?"

"Scavengers," Jake says. "Or marauders!"

Jake's youthful enthusiasm is not particularly infectious in this situation. Funny how easy it is to lose a child's glee for imminent danger. I'm not certain what it says about adults who lose that natural inclination. Or those who maintain it. Or children who are born without it, for that matter.

"Do you think they're going to attack us?" The tinge of fear in tone is palpable. Truant is a wanderer, not a warrior. Not yet.

"I'm not sure. They're herding right now. Six of them, if I'm correct, on three sides." Zeke's calm is no more infectious to Truant than Jake's excitement. I'm not saying Truant is a cookie waiting to crumble. He's simply out of his element, feeling claustrophobic, and without a doubt lacking any control over this situation.

"Don't worry," Jake assures him. "Dad's the best and I'm next." The child winks at Truant, and for just a moment Truant sees the man Jake might grow into.

"How can you tell how many are out there?"

"Eyes and ears," Jake says, answering for his father. "You do not have to see your enemy if you know what you're looking for." This is a trained response, spoken dogmatically as Jake checks his weapons.

"Where do you think they're herding us?"

"Uncertain," Zeke says, throaty tone of steel. "Does not matter. We move accordingly, for the time being in the same direction. Even odds they want nothing to do with us. You have to be careful out here. They may just be escorting us through their territory."

Truant is suspicious Zeke doesn't believe his own words. Hard to say.

"We stay alert. See what happens when we're out of this town."

Relief fills Truant's lungs with a nice deep sigh when they safely exit the industrial complex. Open water fills his eyeballs with a dancing, glistening vista. Nothing follows them out of the city. They continue south throughout the afternoon, Zeke perpetually watching for followers as Truant and Jake chat the day away.

According to Jake, Ezekiel was the best and most feared gunfighter in Detroit. A child from the slums of lower Detroit, Zeke fought his way into the arenas of the Upper City. Men like Zeke were usually sacrificial lambs for polished, sponsored, wealthy gunfighters who rarely challenged one another to death matches. Death was for the poor, while the visage of murderous heroes shown on posters in the bedrooms of children throughout the upper levels. The gunfighters were this generation's biggest sports stars.

Despite his success, Zeke was a villain. He was a denizen of the lower levels who refused sponsorship. A "deviously humble, grotesque abomination" of everything the Professional Gunfighter's Association stands for. What's the point in taking another man's life if you aren't going to revel in the glory, sex, drugs, money, and social status being a triumphant murderer affords you? Seriously. Did the man's life you took mean nothing to you?

The only reason Zeke was allowed to fight in the Upper City was that all of the gunfighters in the professional league wanted a piece of him. Which they got. Zeke had in fact been shot ten times but had never lost. Most of the biggest names would only challenge him to non-lethal duels, but there's a registry of all the men Zeke killed, and hundreds of families, both rich and poor, who hope Zeke burns in hell.

"So after all that time hiding below the city, someone you knew sold you out?"

"Dad says it was bound to happen sooner or later."

"Everyone's desperate in the lower levels," Zeke says. "Whoever did it most likely had no choice. There is an entire division of Detroit's Correctional Patrol devoted to unregistered children. They're property, meant for labor. I was hopeful we might survive a few more years and then sneak away. Let Jake get a little older before we took on this journey."

"I still can't believe I landed next to your boat."

"Strange providence, indeed," says Zeke. There's no suspicion in his voice. Only his face.

"Are the other big cities as bad as Detroit?"

Jake snoozes in the sun while Truant and Zeke toss conversation. That kid's nap-ability is the mark of a profound soul, I promise. You will hear tale of many Jacob Trates, so long as I breathe to tell them, and every version of Jake you meet will know the enduring, pastoral resonance of naptime sleep.

"Most likely. Some better than others, some worse, I would think, as is the nature of things."

"What about the rest of the world?"

"Better than here. I saw news in the Upper City. Learned history, thanks to Jake's mom. When our country fell apart and the cities turned into old world…feudal states…I believe that is the term. Either way, when the United States fell apart the rest of the world continued progress."

"Don't people care about what goes on here? How the poor workers are treated?"

"It is my understanding that much of the world hated the United States before it fell apart. They believe the people here brought this on themselves. Which is true, I suppose, on many levels."

"I just don't understand. People always fight back. They've always fought back."

Zeke answers with a nod, recognition of truth and futility at once. Apt timing for a subject change.

"Hey, Zeke, I think someone's behind us."

"They must have held back. Let us think we were in the clear, then ambush us when there's nowhere to hide."

"What do they want?"

"Everything." Zeke maxes out the throttle then eases back slightly, leaving room for a little burst. "We will not outrun them unless they let us. Jake, up!"

Jake rousts quickly, from asleep to action in an instant (training…).

"Take the rudder. Stay straight."

Zeke pulls a spyglass from a pouch. Six boats – Zeke was correct – gaining fast. Their pursuers' boats aren't much larger than the Trates' but they're sleeker and faster, with hydrofoil skids showing as they hit top speed. There are no flags of gang colors or skulls or crossbones.

"I think I see another town or something!"

Zeke sees Truant point at a distant blur, then lifts the spyglass for a closer look. "Cover ahead, Jake." Collapsing the spyglass and returning it to his satchel, Zeke quickly runs through a weapons check on what, to Truant, is an alarming amount of firearms concealed on his body. Then Zeke retakes the rudder from Jake.

"Ready your weapons."

The assailants fan out, making a move to surround them. Truant's stomach growls. Almost lunchtime.

"Really? Now?"

"Ha ha, I heard that!" says Jake.

"Seriously?"

"Yes! I thought the boat was groaning! Here!" Jake tosses half a bread roll to Truant, bites into the other half, and speaks with his mouth full. "Me too."

"Nerves," says Zeke. "Not a bad thing. Survival instinct. Eat quick. Will help keep your hands steady."

As the other boats close in, Truant clearly makes out the shapes of buildings ahead. Remnants of another city. The assailants tighten formation. They're close enough so Truant can see men and women aboard. Men and women who look nothing like the post-apocalyptic scavengers of the future he'd seen in movies. Their clothes don't look much different than Zeke and Jake's, or his own. No hooting and hollering. No warpaint. Just a bunch of people going about the task at hand.

Jake has returned to the rudder. Large pistols fill both of Zeke's hands.

"Aim to pass between those two buildings on the left, Jake." Just before reaching the first row of old industrial structures, the attackers fully encircle their boat. From about ten meters away, Truant locks eyes with a young blond woman in a boat to his left.

"Hold steady, son."

Mesmerized by the girl, Truant barely hears Zeke, but out of the corner of his eye he sees the gunfighter rise up, arms out wide with pistols at length. Standing tall in the center of their craft, Zeke slowly rotates, as if deciding who to shoot first. The attackers break off pattern in different directions and Jake dives the boat between the two buildings as his father instructed.

"I caught them off guard but they'll regroup!" Zeke shouts to be heard over the roar of boat engines echoing off the buildings. The attackers drop back into formation and continue their pursuit throughout the flooded city as Jake deftly weaves the boat in and out of dilapidated structures. Despite the commotion, Truant notices an old fast food restaurant sign just below the water's surface. His stomach growls again.

"Ridiculous!" Truant shouts at his belly.

"What?" shouts Zeke.

"Nothing! Just…not the time!"

"Here, take this! Just in case!" Zeke pulls out a small gun and tosses it to Truant. Rather than catch it, Truant bats the pistol out of the air and into the water. Zeke's eyes bulge in disbelief.

"What the hell did you do that for?"

"I don't like guns!"

"Well you didn't have to throw it in the damn drink!"

"I wasn't ready and you threw it at me!"

"Alright just get down!"

Zeke opens fire on the other boats as Jake continues weaving in between buildings. Truant worries about the pretty girl and his stomach growls, and he realizes that Zeke is giggling like a mad man as he unloads his weapons, and then as quickly as the shooting began it's over.

Save for the hum of their little boat, everything goes quiet when they fly out of the other side of town. Zeke drops back down to reload, but none of the other boats follow them outside the city. The intimidation demonstration has worked. Truant isn't sure the attackers ever fired back.

They didn't. Whatever their intent, Zeke's maniacal warning scared them off, more safe than sorry. With great intention, Zeke did not wound anyone.

Once again, our three travelers head south in open waters. The shift from chaos to calm takes a moment to absorb before Truant breathes an enormous sigh of relief and refocuses his attention.

Damn, I'm really hungry.

"I'm sorry about your gun."

Our travelers are camped on the roof of an old barn. Still no land in sight but the waters are growing shallow, relatively speaking. A twenty-foot section of the barn's roof is above water, pitched at a comfortable angle for lying on one's back to stargaze. Zeke has barely spoken since the kerfuffle earlier in the day and has said nothing directly to Truant.

"It was a poor decision on my part. No apology is necessary."

"Well, I feel really bad. I've never even held one. I just don't like to hurt things."

"I understand."

Perhaps Jake, young as he is, misses the unspoken dialogue happening between his father and Truant. The eye contact. The facial expressions. The understanding that somewhere between Truant's instinctual aversion to causing pain and the murderous abandon of Zeke's former life, somewhere in there is the answer. Somewhere in there is the accurate measure of one person's right to survive balanced with the respect one should carry for all other life. Perhaps Jake, young as he is, perfectly interprets said unspoken dialogue and has decided his dad and his new best pal need to chill the hell out.

"You should have seen the look on your face when dad threw the gun at you! It was hilarious!"

Truant smiles gingerly at Jake, but isn't sure if it's okay to laugh.

"And you should have seen your face when he smacked it into the water!" Jake continues, pointing at his father, slapping his knee with laughter. A moment's resistance and Zeke joins his son. Then, to Truant's pleasant surprise, Zeke reaches over and playfully smacks him on the side of the head, mussing his hair as a finale. Group laughter removes any tension still clinging to the air, then settles appropriately as the teehees and hoohahs taper off naturally.

"Zeke, do you mind if I ask you a question?"

"Not at all."

"A personal question…"

"Ask."

"What's with the giggling?"

"I'm not certain. It only happens in conflict, I think. I'm barely aware of it. I think the reaction is based in fear. It often scared the water out of my opponents, I can tell you that."

"What about you, Jake? Do you giggle when you shoot?"

"I don't think so. Dad, do I?"

"Not so far."

Zeke goes quiet and trades a thousand-mile stare for activity, beginning to sort out dinner. Jake and Truant chat about the future and the past. Where they're going. Where they are.

They presume to be close to the south end of Ohio. While they eat, Zeke explains they'll be out of deep water soon, heading into marshes that border what's left of dry ground in the North-to-South middle of the country.

That night, Truant lays awake on his back staring at the sky. Stars blink in full force, casting their spell on him. He can't get that pretty girl out of his head, the one on the boat. Can't is fine. He doesn't want to anyway. Months of hiking alone before he met old Curtis Gout at the filling station, and now these two new companions. A long time since he has seen a pretty female. Perhaps the first time he's ever been so bothered by one. She has stirred something in him he's unfamiliar with. If he's felt this before he hasn't noticed, or he paid very little attention, or the feeling wasn't quite this intense. This feels like the flame of a freshly struck match chasing the wood to your thumb. Like race cars in your veins. Like ice cream on your brains.

Maybe tomorrow I'll get Zeke to show me how to shoot. An out-of-character, haphazard thought, barely heard and summarily scoffed at as his mind sinks into a black pool of restful dreams. Dreams never to be remembered, analyzed, or given a froggy shit about.

The following night is the opposite. A restless bitch. Gone is the peaceful slumber of the night before. Truant's dreams are fast, furious, and waking. He runs through them until morning. Sometimes chased, sometimes chasing, always running, and in the morning he's exhausted.

Despite his brain's initial protests, over coffee Truant asks if Zeke will teach him to shoot.

"Jake will show you. It will be a good lesson for you both."

While Zeke preps breakfast, Jake shows Truant what his father has taught him, including mantras designed to instill calm and resolve when faced with conflict. There's no glee in the boy's instruction and Truant marvels over his continued perception of Jake's intermittent manhood.

Properly instructed, Truant fires the gun once and promptly hands it back to Jake.

"Thank you, Jake, but I don't think this is for me."

Zeke takes notice and Truant catches his glance. For Zeke's benefit, he says to Jake, "I'm glad you showed me, just in case. If we get into more trouble, I promise I'll find another way to help."

"Dry goods are low," says Zeke. "Land is close, but I believe we should double time our travel. We'll need to hunt soon."

"I'm sorry, Zeke. You packed for two people. I've made your food run short."

"Don't be sorry. We chose to pull you out of the water. And I've watched you eat. Your respect for the situation is clear. Meanwhile, that one is still chasing a potbelly."

"Hey!"

"He says with a mouth full of food, no less." Zeke motions to his son with a spoon and a smile. "Come here, Truant, and take the till. I'll show you how to control the boat."

On through another day and into the evening. Any plans for shift changes give way to the reality that Zeke is in a constant state of defensive ready, eschewing rest for maintaining the watchful eye.

"You boys should sleep."

Without protest, Jake falls off immediately, lightly snoring and mumbling to the moon. Truant ponders, eyes half-open on Ezekiel. *The portal takes you where you're supposed to go. That's what Curtis said. So why am I here?* A million-dollar question, Truant, often sold for a penny.

Why am I here?

Standing at a urinal? To pee. One cent, please.

No, why am I here? Why do I exist? I'll pay you to tell me, though I'm a little short of a million.

If Curtis doesn't know whether the portal was made by someone or something, or if it's just…natural, how does he know it takes you where you're supposed to go? How does it know it's taking you where you're supposed to go? Is it because that's where you are? You are where you are so that's where you're supposed to be?

That's stupid. There has to be a reason. But that means someone or something is watching me and sent me here? Like a god. Like God? That's stupid too.

Well, which is it, kid? Which is it?

When he left the orphanage, all Truant fully understood was the call to run. That was the extent to which he had contemplated the purpose of his life. Curtis Gout was convinced of some grand scheme, just like many of the people Truant grew up around. If they were all correct, then Truant's parents and sister had been taken from him for a reason. If their death had been a choice, then Truant didn't care for whoever pulled that string.

"Truant," says Zeke, quietly.

"Yes?"

"Would you mind taking the run for a while?"

"Of course not." Truant moves to stern and sits opposite Zeke. "Have you slept at all?"

"Not much. Mostly rest with one eye open, so to speak, but I'm finding it hard to fight right now. I think I might fall out in a minute if you can pilot. Will you stay awake?"

"Yep. No problem. My head's all wrapped up in nonsense right now anyways."

"It wears on your face. Is there anything you might like to talk about, while I'm still here?"

Truant knows Zeke is sincere, and he would enjoy sharing his thoughts with him, but Zeke needs rests.

"Not unless you hold the answers to all the questions of the universe."

"Oh, one of those nights. I have had many, myself. Unfortunately, I do not have all the answers to all the questions of the universe, but I may have some. We may discuss them later if you wish. Right now, however, there is not enough time. The only answer I have for any of those questions is sleep."

"Ha. Sometimes sleep is a superhero."

"Indeed. One question for you if I may, before I fall out."

"Sure thing."

"When you fired Jake's gun?" Moonlight, face, and body language give clear meaning to Zeke's question.

"It scared me. Not the gun exactly. I don't want that type of power." Truant looks to Zeke for understanding, a glimpse of which may have strained the man's face just before his shoulders slump and his chest heaves out a deep breath of slumber.

2

The first arrow lands about three feet behind Truant's left shoulder. The feathers trim his ear as the arrow flies by. He sits confused and beginning to bleed.

Zeke had pulled the boat up to the side of a hill at dusk and tied it to a tree. Excitement over dry land was shared, so they set camp on the side of a hill and had just built a tilted fire to discuss the next day's journey over dinner. Zeke thought they could get one more full day's use out of the boat. After that, they could take a more circuitous route by water or cut a straight path by land. Staying on the boat might be a little faster trip even with the extra distance involved, but they were all sick of the water and the confines of the small craft. Of course, by the time they need another boat, they'll likely be sick and tired of all the walking.

Anyway, Zeke has just said, "So tomorrow should be our last day in the damn thing," when they hear the whistle of the first arrow and Truant's ear suddenly begins to bleed.

The arrows rain down. Zeke is hit in the left shoulder and Jake takes one in the right thigh. Jake's eyes and mouth bulge wide in pain but he doesn't scream. Flying into action, Zeke jumps the fire to land in front of his son.

"Grab your packs and get to the boat!" Zeke draws his weapons and fires shots in all directions. Jake throws water on the fire, engulfing them in smoke for cover. Truant grabs his and Jake's packs and they all make for the boat, stopping short as a wall of arrows blocks their escape.

"Screw the boat! Run!" Turning to follow his own orders, Zeke is hit from behind, square in his left ass cheek. "Son of a bitch!" He grabs Jake and hoists him over his shoulder, tossing his pack to Truant, who is now shouldering all three as they scramble away along the side of the hill.

"Jake, get that thing out of me."

Reaching down from his perch over his father's shoulder, Jake tugs at the arrow in his father's butt, pulling it halfway out before it breaks. Zeke growls.

"You told me to!"

"I'm fine!"

"I'm sorry!"

"Start shooting!"

Arrows hiss by as they maneuver in and out of trees, gingerly maintaining their footing in the hillside mud and brush. Truant leads, continuously regathering and repositioning all of their gear while Zeke fires warning shots into the woods. Jake covers their backs as he bounces around on his father's shoulder. The reports from the gunfire numb Truant's ears, muting all sounds into one of those surreal, "is this really happening" moments, where the loudest noise in your head is your own breath. Something tumbles by in front of him and he skids to a stop, then realizes it was a person. One of Zeke's bullets found a leg, sending an attacker flailing into the water.

Shouts and war yelps give the chase a Hollywood hack-job cowboys and Indians feel, making Truant feel more like a guy trapped in an irresponsible representation loop than a young man adrift in the future. Something that sounds like Zeke's voice warbles behind him. He looks over his shoulder again, to see if Zeke is trying to communicate with him, but all he sees is smoke and gunfire. How are they reloading so fast? Where is all the ammunition coming from?

Zeke bursts forth from behind a tree, zig-zagging and shooting, giggling wildly as he carries his son, attempting to run and shoot while people are shooting arrows at them.

"Did you say something?" yells Truant.

"What?!"

"What did you say?!"

"What?! Nothing! Keep moving! Wait, look out!"

Mouths are moving and words are spoken but Truant still can't hear Zeke. He can't hear himself, but he can see Zeke's face as he's looking over his shoulder while he's running forward on the side of a hill in the woods while people are shooting arrows at him (that's a run-on sentence for a dude who's running, right there…). Truant sees Zeke's expression change and decides he had better have a look in the direction he's moving again, so he turns to catch his eyes up with his body and is met face to face by a stout tree.

Striking the tree head-on while moving as fast as he can for the given terrain, everything goes black as Truant crumples and tumbles, rolling into the water below. Dazed, he sinks for a few moments before his eyes reopen and adjust to murky waters that are shaded by the natural canopy above. Struggling against his own weight and discombobulation, Truant rights himself and climbs back up through the haze, clawing at the submerged land of the hillside, bumping something under the surface of the lake (or river or whatever the hell you would call it) that doesn't feel natural. Groping his way around the shape, he discovers an opening, an entrance to something, and swim-crawls inside. Several yards from the entrance, water dissipates and the tunnel opens into a large cavern.

Truant's head breaks the surface of the water, eyes in search of his companions. Crouched by a large tree, Zeke and Jake are intermittently shooting into the woods and searching the water for their lost companion.

"I'm here!"

"C'mon, let's go!" Zeke shouts. "Get out of there!"

"No! I found something! Follow me!"

From ten feet up the side of the hill, without argument, Zeke picks Jake up and throws him into the water, then jumps in himself. Miscalculating the distance or his own ability to leap, Zeke clears most of the ground but not quite all, landing hard just in front of the water. Sharply turning his ankle, he falls in with a grunt and a splash.

"There's a hole in the ground! Swim!" Truant grabs Jake and shoves him underwater toward the entrance. Zeke gathers himself and heads for the entrance, shoving Truant ahead of him. Arrows slip through the water in their general direction but within a few moments, they're safely inside.

The cavern, as it turns out, is an old mine shaft prep room. There's barely visible light, just the dim glow of scattered sunlight reflecting through the dirty waters into the first few feet of the room. The type of glowing darkness you can only see when looking from the vantage point of a greater darkness.

Our three companions crouch against a wall, the Trates with their gun barrels trained on the entrance. Zeke with an arrow sticking out of his shoulder and half an arrow protruding from his buttocks. Jake with one in his leg.

Silence, until Zeke feels assured that they haven't been followed. "I think we are safe, for a time."

Fishing a dry box from his pack, Truant strikes a match, cupping it in his hands long enough to find some old rags scattered across dryer areas of the room. Three torches are fashioned in the near darkness. Further into the room, they discover old lanterns hanging on the wall next to an offshoot tunnel entrance. Truant works with the lanterns, lighting those still capable of burning while Zeke tends to the arrow in Jake's leg.

"Bite down. This will be sharp."

Wet and weary, huddled around a very small fire. Smoke drifts from the room, bobbing and weaving in the vacuum pull of the internal shaft entrance. After Zeke bandages Jake's leg, Jake takes his turn mending his father. Zeke will never say it, but Truant is fairly certain the man found getting shot in his buttocks rather humiliating (if not the wound itself, his son mending his rump…).

The arrow in Zeke's shoulder cut all the way through. Truant has to help Jake pull it out the back. Another arrow had found Zeke's arm, and though he jerked it out on the run, the arm bled freely until Jake was able to bandage it as well. Then there's Zeke's ankle, sprained fiercely when he attempted his jump into the water. Now it's the size of a grapefruit.

Jake's leg is another issue. Best guess, based on the depth of the arrow's shaft that was in Jake's leg, muscle was torn and the arrowhead may have hit bone. Despite the boy's courage in deal-ing with the pain, Truant wonders if he'll be able to walk. Or fight off infection, for that matter. Who knows what disease or bacte-ria is in the damn water they swam through?

Both of the Trates are badly hobbled and there sits the lucky teenager from the past, nary a scratch (though he *had* already been shot once since arriving in the future). Yes, Truant's ear was sliced wide open near the top, and it is a gash that will never fully heal, but living with a split ear for the rest of his life pales in com-parison to the scope of matters at hand. His companions are both in need of legitimate medical care. They are basically trapped un-derground. For all they know, they could be sitting in an entrance to caverns their attackers control. And who were they, anyway, shooting friggin' arrows at them? Was it the same people from the boats?

Truant wonders if that girl is with them.

"We'll sleep here tonight, obviously. In the morning I will take the tunnel further into ground, see where it leads. Most likely it will come to some form of dead end where the mining halted, in which case we'll have to go back out the way we came. If that is our path, we'll need to rest here as long as possible to heal. I can run on this leg if I have to but it would not be wise for a few days." Zeke pokes at his ankle with a grimace, almost as if he's chastising it for being weak. "Our food supply is low. And there is Jake's leg, which will be stiff and swollen by morning. His movement will also be limited, and we cannot fight on the run like that again. We're lucky they weren't with guns. We would not have survived."

"I'll be fine," Jake says.

"Yes, you will." Zeke smiles at his son's spirit.

"At least our gear is dry," Jake continues. "That's one mark in our favor." When you live on the water, you prepare for certain things, like wetness. The Trates' packs are waterproofed on the inside. Truant's on the other hand… For the second time since arriving in the future, his pack is soaked through. Its contents are strewn about the floor of the mine for drying. "Oh, sorry." A sheepish little grin washes Jake's face.

"Ha. No worries," says Truant. "You guys got the stuff that needs to stay dry. Worst thing I might lose is a notebook full of nonsense. But listen, Zeke, let me go into the tunnels. I'm not hurt. I can move faster, and you need to rest your leg as much as possible."

"Unless you agree to take a weapon, I think it is best that I go, bad leg or no. You're a courageous sort, perhaps graced, but we don't know what's down there."

"What's graced?" asks Jake.

"Big Black Book stuff. Now isn't the time, son, but remember the question."

"Zeke, I don't need a gun to go down there. If something happens I can yell, and I can run if I have to and you can't."

"True, but if I go in and something happens you will know immediately. The crack of a gunshot travels far and fast, and you will have time to prepare for whatever happens next, most likely a quick exit back up through the water. This is not open for debate. You have free will so you may choose your own path, but if you go in we all go in, 'cause I won't let you go in unprotected, possibly drawing danger our direction with no warning for us, and I won't leave my son here alone. And if we all go in we may very well find ourselves trapped. So, I ask you to consider my logic, and we will sleep on it, and in the morning we will see what we see."

Truant doesn't need to sleep on it, he knows Ezekiel is right. The sensation that Zeke is beginning to feel protective of him gives Truant comfort. He is, after all, about as far away from home as a young man can get.

Good thing too, that he doesn't need to sleep on Zeke's words, because his mind refuses him a peaceful rest yet again. The girl from the boat is back, only this time they're in the past. Truant and his mystery lady are caveman and cavewoman but from different tribes, and their tribes are at war with each other, and the kid has never even read Romeo and Juliet.

A great battle rages between the tribes. Everyone is throwing spears and stones except Truant. He refuses to throw the rocks. The caveman to his left keeps handing Truant rocks and Truant keeps handing them to the caveman on his right. Then he feels a sharp pain in his chest and falls to the ground. When he looks down there's a spear sticking out of him. Impaled directly through the heart, he looks back up to see the pretty girl standing above him. Taking the handle of the spear, she twists and twists, all the while smiling the most lovely smile. And she's so beautiful. He says it again, She's so beautiful. *You're so beautiful.* And somewhere his universal self, who floats above his dreams and watches his sleepy self take part in his dreams, his universal self keeps saying the same thing over and over: *Wake up, stupid.* But he doesn't wake up. On the floor of the mine his body tosses and turns. Inside his mind, the spear keeps twisting.

"I will be back as soon as possible." Zeke is adjusting the splint he's fashioned for his ankle. "I'm going to leave before Jake is up. It's easier. If something happens – it won't – but if it does, and I don't come back, don't come after me. If there is something down there that can keep me from returning to my son, there will be nothing the two of you can do about it. Take Jake and get the hell out of here. I don't know where to tell you to go, other than where we were already heading."

"I'll try, but I'm not sure I can make Jake do anything."

"If the time comes, figure it out." Zeke pauses for a moment. "There was a look you had on your face the other night, I've seen it in the mirror. I'm not the trusting sort, but I trust you. You have a good spirit, Truant, and I believe in things we do not see. One of those things tells me, makes me wonder, if we aren't somehow family, and together for a reason."

Truant expects more, hoping Zeke might speculate further. Instead, the gunfighter stands and checks the presence of each weapon on his body.

"I'll be back."

Once Zeke is out of sight, Truant shakes his head with a chuckle and says, "I'll be back," in that most famous of accents.

Jake snores.

That kid can sleep, Truant thinks, watching and waiting for Jake to wake up. What Zeke said about being family. What if Truant were an ancient relative? *How cool would it be if Zeke is my great,*

great, great, great grandson or something like that? What year did he say this is? How many greats would that be? I guess I could be Jake's mom's ancestor instead. Still cool, but not as cool 'cause it sounds like her family kind of sucks.

Quickly growing tired of being alone, Truant decides to warm a little food in the hopes it will wake his younger companion. The food stock disheartens him. Even if Zeke doesn't return (which Truant doesn't want to consider), he and Jake will run out of food soon, so he only cooks enough for the kid. The plan works, as the smell of breakfast rousts Jake from his slumber.

"Where's my dad?"

"He already left."

"He's a sneak."

"He'll be back before you know it." Truant hands Jake a tin bowl holding a thin egg mix and dried bacon.

"Where's yours?"

"Already ate." He had actually taken a bite while cooking so he wouldn't have to lie. A half-truth, perhaps, but not a lie. Truant hates lies. Not real big on half-truths either, but this is an uncommon situation. "You love sleep and food. I just can't figure which one you love more."

"Both!" Jake shows an open-mouth smile then shoves a spoon of food in for effect, giggling as he chews. "Do you think we should go after my dad?"

"How often do you disobey your father, Jake?

"Never."

"Do you think now is a good time to start?" Truant wants to go as well. Completely shaking the fear that Zeke may not return is a tall order, putting his emotional state in some form of denial: Stay the course and everything will be okay.

"I don't want to sit here all day waiting on him to come back. It's going to make me psycho."

"Okay then, we won't just sit around waiting on him. I have an idea."

"What?"

"We're going to make history."

"How are we going to make history?"

"Have you ever heard of hieroglyphics? Or cave drawings?" Despite growing up in Texas, Truant received a solid public education.

"No. Say that again."

"Hieroglyphics."

"Hie...ro...glyphics."

"Yep. All the way back to the days when people lived in caves, before they even spoke to each other with words, they would record their history on the walls of the caves where they lived and tombs where they buried people. They would draw pictures of wars, and gods, and people being sacrificed, and babies being born, and famines, and droughts, and anything that would happen to them. Then, when the Egyptians came along, they used pictures to represent an actual language. So, instead of the drawings just showing things that happened, the pictures actually represented specific words."

"What do you mean by people being sacrificed?"

For a moment, but only a moment, Truant chastises himself for mentioning human sacrifice to a child, then thinks, *The kid's packing heat, dude. He was literally in a gunfight yesterday.* "A long time ago they used to kill people because they thought it would make their gods happy, or bring rain for their crops, or help them win battles with other people."

"That's stupid."

"Yes it is. People can be pretty stupid. But, cave drawings and hieroglyphs are cool. They're history. We can draw on these walls, and someday, even a hundred years from now or more, someone might find them."

"That's pretty awesome."

"Exactly. So, you want to help me make history or not?"

"Yes, but I'm not very good at drawing."

"That doesn't matter, goofball. Do you think cavemen were good artists? I'm terrible at drawing, but that's what makes this so cool. It will look like someone did it thousands of years ago." The idea of leaving a historical mark on the future has Truant genuinely enthusiastic.

"What's a goofball?"

"You, you're a goofball. Kids are goofballs. Running in circles until you fall down. Laughing with food in your mouth. Farts. All goofball behavior."

"I'm a gunfighter."

"Yeah, you're complicated, but you're still a goofball."

"You're a goofball."

"Yes I am."

"What are we gonna draw?"

"We're gonna draw our story. You do the beginning. You can start with leaving your home, and then I can help with the stuff after I came along. We can even put it on two different walls if we want to."

"What are we going to draw with?"

"The same things the cavemen did. We can use rocks to scrape, and soot from the fire, and this might sound a little gross, but they used blood and you and I have got plenty of that."

"That's not gross, that's awesome!" exclaims Jake, immediately tugging at his bandages.

I often ponder the mindset of the young, specifically myself as a youngster. Our ability for frivolity. For distraction. For compartmentalization. Fair to say, I believe, that any of those measures along with many, many more, may increase or decrease as we age into adulthood. Depending, of course, on the individual. However, the thing I ponder the most is the accuracy of my own memory. As an adult, are we truly capable of staying in touch with the child we were, or is our perception too skewed by age and experience? In other words, do I remember my world as a child honestly, or has the truth of my youth been stolen from me by growth?

Who's to say? How can we be certain, one way or the other? I don't believe we can.

One thing I can be certain of: Truant and Jake spend the afternoon drawing their adventure on the walls of the mine shaft. The work takes their minds off Zeke's absence, as designed, consuming them to the point of revelry, falling into such a state of artistic bohemia that they begin to grunt and move about as they imagine cavemen would, fighting over rocks and good sticks to draw with and then falling out with laughter.

"Do you think anyone will ever see this?" asks Jake, surveying their work.

"Absolutely, Jake. We just made history."

The worry in Jake's eyes has reached its apex when Zeke finally limps back into the cavern. Truant isn't certain how long Zeke has been gone, losing track of time by design with his and Jake's artistic endeavor, but his growling stomach and Zeke's countenance affirm it is late in the day. Zeke is obviously weary, and his limp is much worse than when he departed that morning.

"Dad!" Jake rushes to Zeke's side, briefly wrapping his arms around his father before stepping back with a face full of questions. "What did you see? Where does it go? Anywhere good?"

"Give your old man a minute to sit down and rest his legs." Zeke settles on the ground and removes the splint from his leg, then his boots. The damaged ankle is so bruised the skin has almost turned black, and the swelling has worsened.

"Why don't you let me re-wrap that?" says Truant, wondering how much pain Zeke is in.

"Let it breathe for a minute, then yes, thank you. It will need a tight wrap to fight the swelling." Stretching his legs and toes, Zeke takes a few slugs from his canteen as he soaks in Jake's and Truant's cave paintings. "What's all this?"

"The passage of time," says Truant, feeling clever. To his surprise, Zeke rattles off a full-throated laugh.

"Is that right? Good you boys stayed busy."

"Would you just tell us what you saw?" Jake pleas. "I'm losing my patience."

"Alright, alright," Zeke chuckles. "That path leads far into the ground, and deep. To look at the walls, it appears the tunnel was mined as it was dug. Eventually, the tunnel comes to what I believe was once a dead end, where I found another passageway. The second passage appears newer than the original mine. The cutting is different, and the walls aren't stripped of minerals. And the support structure is thatch work. The second tunnel is as long as the first, and though newer, doesn't appear recently traveled. Large portions have collapsed where the thatch has degraded. I had to dig out some areas and crawl to keep going, which ate much of the day, but eventually the path cleared. If we go back in, we should make better time than my first run."

"But what did you find?"

"Patience, son. I'm not finished."

"I'm sorry."

"It's okay, I understand your excitement. To answer your question, I eventually came to another small open space where the trail split in three directions. Three new possibilities for travel. This is when I decided to turn back. The way I see it, those trails are new enough there's a possibility they happened after the flood, or at least right beforehand. Either way, I figure any of those three paths will take us somewhere. They weren't a part of the original mine, so I don't suspect they will dead end. Otherwise, it would have been senseless to build them. The question is, do we travel further inside, or take our chances back above ground? The problem we must consider when trying to answer that question is we are almost out of food. We lost supplies when we fled the boat. We either eat tonight or in the morning, and then we are pickled."

"You said pickled."

"Yes, I did. Is this a saying in your time?

"Yeah. I know someone else who used to say that. I'm sorry I interrupted. Go on, please."

"Once again, we have two choices, go back outside and risk attack to find food, or travel into the tunnels and hope they safely lead to some sort of food and clean water source before we pass out from hunger and exhaustion. Personally, I would prefer a heads-up fight than dying of hunger."

"Me too," says Jake, instinctively agreeing with his father.

"Zeke, what about fish?"

Why haven't our friends already considered fishing? Well, to be fair, running out of food is a recent conversation. Also, Zeke and Jake aren't traveling with fishing gear. Frankly, I'm not certain man or boy has ever dropped a bait, despite their previous living conditions below Detroit. Truant has a line and a hook that he's used leisurely, fishing a sunny day away for a one man, one trout buffet. Not much help if trying to rapidly catch enough fish to supply three appetites for several days while also avoiding a potential attack from futuristic marauders. However, a pair of pants knotted at the ankles can make a functional net.

With a plan in place and all hunger futures invested in fishing stocks, Zeke decides they may as well go to bed with full bellies in hopes of a good night's rest. Truant cooks most of what food is left, and while he prepares the meal Jake explains their cave drawings to his father. After dinner, Zeke gives in to Jake's persistence and agrees to add his day's adventure to the walls. Jake and Truant do most of the actual artwork, but Zeke helps. Historically accurate, Zeke's portion is a fairly mundane portrayal of crawling and walking through a cave.

That night, with sleep stalking him, the pretty young lady from the boat shows up again. Not in Truant's dreams. Not this time. A vision of her appears in his mind's eye before slumber. A memory of her face in the past. He's seen her before. That's right. Yes! The barn. Holy cows! If he's seen her before, he might see her again. Something's going on here and she's part of it. Open arms and glowing heart, the vision invites him in, wrapping herself around him like a warm blanket, rocking him to sleep.

The next morning, Jake and Zeke are up and chatting softly as Truant escapes the sandman. He shuffles over to them sitting by their burner, boiling water. Three mugs are ready, each with a brown powder waiting in the bottom before Zeke pours the water over. The mix tastes like bitter chocolate and root but isn't heavy. The water remains as thin as if nothing was stirred into it.

"What is this?"

"Tumah Tea," replies Zeke. "It is for health, and energy."

"It's made from ground animal teeth and bones," adds Jake. "And chocolate beans and tea leaves."

"Interesting. It sounds like it should taste so much better than it does."

Jake giggles.

"No one knows exactly what this is made of," says Zeke, "except the witches who make it, and anyone who asks a witch for their recipe is a fool if they believe what they are told. But it does good work to a body, and it will help sustain us until we eat again."

"Well, let's hope it's fish for lunch because this is disgusting."

"I like it," says Jake, eliciting two very disbelieving stares. "What? I do."

Zeke just shakes his head and Truant says, "Zeke, did you say witches?"

"Bad choice of words when speaking to a time traveler, I suppose. I simply meant practitioners of old-world medicine."

"Very old-world, by the taste of it. An old, old, terrible tasting world," says Truant, gulping down the rest of his mug's contents.

"Oh," says Zeke. "Wait, you shouldn't…"

Truant's hair suddenly stands straight up. Metaphorically. Metaphorically. Perhaps a single hair Alfalfa's an alarm, but the sudden acute saucering of his pupils tells the real tale.

"You should have said that before I drank it," mutters Truant, rapidly, brain caught somewhere between an ice cream freeze and a methamphetamine scream.

"The taste," says Zeke. "Usually the taste slows people down."

"You look crazy!" says Jake.

"I feel crazy."

"That won't last long," says Zeke. "You will slow down soon."

"Well, why wait? I suppose now is as good as time as any." Truant stands and removes his clothing down to a cruddy pair of boxer shorts. "You know, I'm definitely in need of a bath as it is. These shorts can probably walk on their own now. Have you guys got any soap?"

Even Zeke laughs at Truant's sudden, fast-talkiness.

"What?" asks Truant, knotting his pants legs at the bottoms to form a makeshift net. "What's so funny? Am I talking fast? I'm talking fast. Why aren't you?"

Both Trates show their mugs, still mostly full of Tumah.

"Oh sure, of course. Oh well. What's done is done. Now all we have to do is hope I can sneak up on an unsuspecting school of fish while I'm all jacked up on some sort of freaky future speed." Heading back towards the tunnel leading to the water, Truant continues rambling until out of earshot. "What's this? It's tea? It tastes terrible but you should drink it anyway. Drink it and see what happens. What do you mean see what happens? You'll see. Just drink the tea. But not too fast. Oh noooooo…don't drink it too fast…"

A lack of visibility is the most likely hang-up to Truant's plan, but the sun shines brightly as he enters the water. Dirty lake water still, certainly, but the early morning sun's piercing glow cuts through tree coverage and highlights the movement of blurred objects. Several feet from the mine's entrance, Truant releases most of the air in his lungs, sinking to a shallow bottom. He holds the net out as he sinks, passively catching several fish along the way. Once his feet hit bottom, he methodically scoops the net down and horizontally in one slow, sweeping motion. The process is slow, as he can't stay underwater long without oxygen, but the method allows him to cast his net without stirring up a huge commotion and scaring all the fish away (the same reason all three travelers had agreed one fisherman was the best likely scenario for what Truant is attempting).

After his first scoop, he gently pushes off the underwater floor, easing back towards the surface, rather than swimming all the way back into the mine. Leary of potential attackers, he eases his head out of the water near debris and brush, scanning the area. Remember, the surface runs a steep incline into this water.

Truant lays at an angle, keeping his body in the water from the neck down, and scoops out a decent sized hole in the dirt just above the water's edge, then dumps in the contents of his pants-net. Not much of a catch to look at, but Truant wards off any disappointment, takes a deep breath, and sinks back into the water for another run.

This pattern goes on for some time, until the midday sun begins to shift its light from Truant's fishing area. The catch thus far is meager. Genuinely disappointing, to be blunt. Truant is growing exhausted and hungry, and the contents of his dirt cooler aren't watering his lips. A meal in there, perhaps two, but nothing to write home about or plan a spelunking tour with.

One more pass and successive last gasp of hope, at least for the day. Fortune often smiles on persistence, as Truant sinks right in front of a school of fish. Moving fast and swimming straight at him, Truant opens his pants-net to best-case-scenario glory. One wiggly sneak swims up his shorts. Surprised, tickled, and slightly scared, Truant wiggles about, somehow actually netting more fish.

The moment passes, and as he binds the pants to keep his catch from escaping, still floating in a swirl of fish, he suddenly understands why he got so lucky. They're fleeing a predator. Whatever is hunting them rams Truant in the chest. He yelps in surprise, losing what little oxygen there is left in his lungs and taking a mouthful of nasty water.

Something wraps itself around his leg as he struggles for the entrance to the mine. Just before he's about to black out he washes into the tunnel. Truant crawls forward, gasping for air, then rises and attempts to run. Holding the pants full of fish out before him, some crazy thing wrapped around his leg, Truant screams bloody murder as he stiff-leg hobble-runs through the shaft.

Truant must be a sight to the Trates as he runs into the mine, soaking wet, dragging a leg with some strange thing wrapped around it and a pair of jeans held out in front of him like a bomb powered by wiggly fish.

"Get it off, get it off, get this damn thing off of me!" Truant tosses the pants full of fish to the floor then dives onto the ground, he and the pants both flopping around as he wrestles with whatever is on his leg.

Jake gets to him first.

"Hold him down!" says Zeke.

Jake grabs Truant by the shoulders and holds him down firmly. Surprisingly firmly considering his age and stature. Zeke grabs the snake-like thing, wrenching it from Truant's leg and smacking it hard against the ground until it stops moving.

"Are you bit?" Zeke asks.

"I'm not sure."

"Check," Zeke says, examining Truant's leg at the same time.

"Here." The thing had attached itself to the inside of Truant's thigh, above the knee. Zeke holds the leg down awkwardly and bends to suck any poison from the wound, but Truant flinches and knees Zeke in the face.

"Lay still," Jake says. "It might have been poisonous."

Zeke, whose mouth is now bleeding on its own, forces Truant's leg still and goes back to work.

"Sorry, Zeke, I'm sorry…"

Zeke sits up and spits out a mouthful of blood, goes in for one more round, then sits back and looks at Truant with a cannibal clown's smile.

"It's okay, my young friend. At least I know you've got a fighting spirit."

"What was that thing?" Truant asks while Zeke and Jake bandage his wound.

"Looks like some kind of eel," says Zeke. "Perhaps a young one."

"It scared the crap out of me."

"We could see that," says Jake, with a teasing lilt.

"And it almost drowned me."

"Would you like a prize?" asks Zeke.

"Oh, okay. Ganging up on me now. Yes. Yes, I would. I would like a prize."

"How about the arrow that was stuck in dad's butt? You can have that."

Zeke snorts, surprised by his son. Jake stares down Truant, stone faced and very pleased with himself. When the teenager from the past finally breaks, all three donate their wind to howling laughter.

"I didn't know there were eels in the middle of America," says Truant as he chews another piece of the well-cooked monster.

"Well," Zeke said, "the land has been flooded for many years now. There is no telling what species have made their way inland."

"Right. I guess if they weren't here before they certainly could be now."

"You're lucky it wasn't a shark," mumbles Jake through a full mouth.

"I guess I am."

After they stuff themselves on eel Asada al Fuego, Truant swims out to collect the rest of the fish he had stored in the hole on the surface. No need to let what's up there go to waste. Meanwhile, Jake and Zeke start cleaning the fish deposit in the cave. They spend the evening preparing for the next phase of their journey. That night before bed, Truant and Jake mark the day's excitement on the walls of the cave.

Truant doesn't sleep well. He's on trial for murder. A frog presides over the court, giving instructions to a jury full of fish. A turtle performs bailiff duties. Dead and zombied, the eel that attacked Truant acts as the prosecutor.

All Truant offers in defense is an apology, sincerely repeated over and over but clearly not enough for absolution from his victims or his own conscience. He's accused of hate crimes. In an unapparelled break from decorum, the frog judge offers him a plea bargain, if only he'll rat out his accomplices and promise never to harm another creature again. Truant declines, pragmatically, and is summarily found guilty by the jury, who never even leave the courtroom to deliberate. A death sentence is conferred. The turtle bailiff shakes his head in disgust while the eel prosecutor poses for cameras and reporters, exclaiming how justice is being served as the executioner throws the switch to an underwater electric chair.

Truant wakes with a shock and a cold sweat, then sighs deeply with relief as he remembers his dream. He sits up and sees Ezekiel staring at him with questioning eyes.

"Bad dreams?"

"Stupid ones."

"Breakfast in the tin there. Should still be warm. Coffee too."

"Sweet. Where's Jake?"

"Morning business."

"That's two days in a row he's been up before me."

"He's always been inconsistent with his sleep. I think that's part of the reason he can sleep anywhere. When it hits, he goes."

"Reminds me of my dad. One of the things I can remember, anyway."

"I've been meaning to ask…family? Friends? more of your story, if you would like to share."

Breakfast is consumed first (eel is not as tasty in the morning…), then Truant briefly discusses losing his parents and a sister in a car crash when he was somewhere around the age Jake is now. After his parents were gone, he grew up in his godmother's foster home. Two older siblings, brothers, were off at different colleges but kept close tabs on him. Until Truant took off on foot, that is, and in this moment, for the first time since leaving Texas on his adventure, Truant realizes what he's done to them. He's correct. They're both worried sick, but what they're going through trying to find out if their little brother is alive, that's another story for another day.

The thought ushers guilty silence and a hung chin. When Truant looks up again, he quietly watches Zeke and Jake pack ammunition.

Zeke is teaching Jake, but it's a retread lesson Jake has clearly heard before. Repetition is the point.

The bullets are laid out on a material akin to aluminum foil. The shells are of various sizes but the same general shape, made from a synthetic material and finished with blunted tips. Father and son work in tandem, Zeke handling a pliable, putty-like substance and Jake capping. Between you and me, the bullet tips are purposefully designed by Zeke to reduce piercing. He also cuts the ignition element's volatility, in effort to make the projectiles less deadly. One large pouch of ammo, already pressed and stowed in Zeke's gear, holds more lethal ammunition. The goal is for that pouch to never be opened.

After the ammo is prepped, the guns are next. Seven firearms are laying in pieces in front of Zeke. Four in front of Jake. Truant watches the Trates clean and reassemble the weapons with a morbid fascination born of his own disdain for violence and his genuine belief that the Trates have no desire to hurt anyone. Indeed, their physical expressions are nothing if not somber.

Where is the line drawn between the right to defend your physical being and protecting your eternal soul? Is there a universal maxim, or is it up to the individual to decide, or is the universal maxim that a moral quandary such as this must be up to the individual? And who says we have souls? And if we don't have souls, does it really matter? Does anything? And if nothing matters, should we just rape this world for all we want until we die?

Whoa. That thought tornado spirals quickly out of control. Truant shakes his head clear and suspends deliberations until further notice as the Trates' meditations over their weapons come to an end. Two of Zeke's pistols go into his pack. The other five are stowed on his body. One on each hip, one on a belt in the middle of his back, one under his left arm connected to that same belt, and one on the inside of his leg strapped to his boot. That one is the smallest and most resembles a gun from Truant's own time. I won't fetishize the others with detailed descriptions, but they look very different than any guns Truant has seen before, though surely mechanisms of the same intent. Death. The wielding of unnatural force to harm another. Perhaps man's greatest sin, and you know that saying about the sins of a father…?

Jake's weapons are stored in his pack, per Zeke's orders. Looking back, remembering that day, I'm obliged to convince myself that Zeke hated those weapons. He hated their cause for existence, the folly of man, and the unfortunate insistence of a cruel world that his son might need those weapons to survive. Looking back, I'm convinced Zeke wanted nothing to do with those goddamn guns.

Anyway, once the Trates are finished and everyone's gear is repacked for travel, they tamp their fire and head into the tunnel.

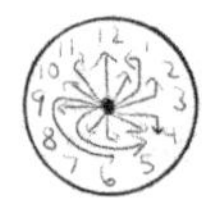

Making their way to the three tunnel entrances where Zeke previously ended his recon takes longer than anticipated. His swollen ankle still hobbles him, and the path he partially dug through two days earlier is more of an obstacle with all three of them crawling together. Zeke leads, followed by Jake with Truant the last. As Zeke manipulates the loose ground in front of him to make his way through, it creates a roadblock for Jake and so on to Truant, slowing their pace.

Jake's wounded leg is snared and reopened by a rock jutting up from the ground, forcing them to stop. They treat and re-bandage the leg as best they can in the cramped tunnel, then agree to food and half an hour of rest. Though Zeke doesn't say it, the rest is mostly for Truant, who appears to be getting sick.

The cold sweat Truant woke up with has stuck with him, inciting shivers throughout the morning. By lunch, he's clearly suffering a fever.

"I'm sure it's just from being all soggy yesterday and the cold air down here," Truant says, but in his heart he fears much worse. His body is reporting to him and it does not bear good news.

Silence, as our companions now sit in front of three tunnel entrances. Zeke has suggested they meditate, listening for winds and sounds, trying to pick up on any sense of vibration for a clue as to which tunnel they should take. After a while he decides to bed down for the evening.

"Here." Zeke hands Truant a warm mug. "Hopefully this will help your fever."

"Thank you." Truant sniffs the concoction, then takes a sip that makes his taste buds wince. Woof, this is worse than the Tumah. "Any idea how we're going to decide which way to go?"

"One. Trial and error. I was hoping for a natural clue, of course. Breeze or sound. Without that our choices are guesswork. I have marked our direction, where we came from and where we have arrived, and the turns in between. If I'm correct, I believe the entrance to the right is the most in line with the hillside entrance you first discovered. If possible, we should proceed in the direction that keeps us closest to the outside world. We obviously have no idea what turns these tunnels may take once we're in them, but the entrance to the right may be the most logical first option.

"What if we each went a little way down a different tunnel?" asks Jake. "We might see something that tells us which one is the best."

"That could save us time, son, but I prefer we remain together. We have no idea what's down here. We do it one tunnel at a time, as a unit. No one will get lost or harmed that way."

While Jake and Zeke prepare food (aka, some type of fish…), Truant wanders back to the entrances of the tunnels. He takes a few steps inside each entrance, just far enough so he can ignore Jake and Zeke's conversation, pondering the tunnel's direction and eventual outcome, both physically and metaphysically. Feeling. Searching for a feeling.

Honestly, our time traveler and/or possible dimension jumper doesn't expect anything to come of his sensory-wielding efforts, but he wanted to be alone for a minute or two anyway. The fever has given him a foggy brain, and yet, the quiet works. As he stands in the "last" tunnel, a notion that was previously engaged in a mental game of hide-and-seek springs forth from behind a tree in his mind. Ta da!

Truant walks back over near the Trates and grabs his backpack.

"Food's almost ready," says Jake.

"Nice," Truant replies, on the move.

"Something amiss?" asks Zeke.

"Just a thought. I'll be right back."

Returning to the tunnel entrances, Truant drops his pack and digs around, retrieving the plastic box that holds Curtis' brother's watch.

Robert Alexander Gout. Bobby. Bobby Gout. That's Curtis Gout's brother. Now I don't have to keep typing "Curtis' brother's watch." As a matter of fact, from this point forward, it's Truant's watch. Curtis gave it to him. It's Truant's now. That's even easier.

Truant opens the box and removes the watch, then holds it out in front of himself. Nothing. Stepping into the entrance on the left, he walks several feet inside. Then several more, until there is almost no residual light from their camping area. A few more steps and Truant is shrouded in darkness when a faint glow appears from the watch.

No kidding? Curtis, I love you.

Hunch summarily justified, Truant retreats from the tunnel. Further utilization of scientific method required (said in robot nerd voice). And holy cow! I just realized this is the point in the story where method meets magic (said in my nerd voice). Huzzah!

Into the middle tunnel, stepping forward towards complete darkness, the watch glows more loudly this time. Bright enough so that he can see the watch's arms. Having previously frozen on an hour of unknown significance to Curtis and Bobby Gout's cosmic entanglement, now all the hands were pointing in one unified direction. Straight ahead. As a trial, Truant turns back towards camp. The hands rotate, maintaining their course down the tunnel.

Quickly out of the middle tunnel and into the entrance on the far right, hypothesizing on the way, Truant's hastily conceived theory is immediately proven correct. In the third tunnel, the watch glows dimly as it had in the first.

"Guys! Come check this out! You gotta see this!"

"Considering we have no other method of navigation, it's as good as any direction to begin with."

"You've got a magic watch! Awesome!" Jake's enthusiasm for the entire situation jumps up several notches when Truant showed the Trates what he discovered. Kids love magic. It's a fact.

"I'm glad you feel that way, Zeke," says Truant, strapping the watch to his wrist. "I know I can't explain it, but I spent a lot of time with Curtis before I got here. This has to be a sign."

"Irrefutably, it is a sign, one way or another, though I'm not certain it's magic." Zeke smiles at his son. "It's possible there are elements in the watch's mechanics that are reacting to chemicals or minerals in the walls or in the air itself to create the glow."

"But what about the hands, dad? They're acting like a compass."

"Yes, but that could be magnetism, just as a normal compass works."

"But our compass doesn't work down here! Don't spoil the fun."

"Our compass works, but with no relevance. Choosing north or south means nothing in a maze unless you know where the exit lies."

"I said not to spoil the fun."

"I thought we agreed that learning is fun?"

"He's got you there, Jake."

"Uh uh. Maybe he got you but not me. Learning *is* fun, and wizards have to *learn* magic. They don't just get to do magic without learning first. Magic is learning and that's a magic watch."

"Zeke, I think he just zinged us both"

"Don't zing your elders, boy."

Jake's fascination with the situation will not be denied. Frankly, he's simply expressing what they're all feeling, the levels of which are appropriately tempered by age and experience. Truant's outer wow factor is reduced by his time at the filling station and all that he saw while there. Zeke's by adulthood.

As they lay down for the evening, Jake can't be turned off. What a mystery! Not only is Truant from the past but he has a magic watch! Appropriate catalyst for extended conversation on mystical subjects. General mystical intrigue and conversational rabbit holes eventually lead to Big Black Book stuff, which Truant learns is a catch-all phrase the Trates use when discussing matters of religion, philosophy, mysticism, and et-cetera, etcetera.

"I've read several religious texts cover to cover. Philosophies as well. Jake's mother's greatest gifts to me were my son and books. I was an intelligent but ignorant man before my time with her. But, to answer your question, I have faith in a higher power no text or man has yet explained to me. Nor will they ever."

"I like that," says Truant, before succumbing to a coughing fit. When the coughing stops, he says. "I read some Bible, but not much. In my time, they preach it to you. I don't care for that."

"What do you mean, preach?" asks Jake.

"I mean people go to buildings and listen to a man or a woman explain life to you and tell you how you are supposed to behave. Other religions too." Cough, cough. "Not at the same building. I mean, all the religions have their own buildings where people go to worship their god."

"That's weird," says Jake.

"Interesting," says Zeke. "I can't imagine the presumption of ex-plaining a text filled with so much contradiction. There are significant themes for one to ponder, but so much absurdity and violence."

"Exactly. In my time people argued about it constantly. They don't fight about it here?"

"Perhaps, in the upper levels there are debates, but I never witnessed what I would call worship. I'm not sure about the rest of the world, but religious books are no longer in print here. No books, for that matter. Not for anyone living below the upper levels. Those in charge, they've scrubbed as much history as possible from the common people. Books, religion, education, all illegal in the lower levels. The poor have only work and exhaustion."

"I can understand why you wanted to escape, even if Jake wasn't too soft to go work in a factory."

"Hey!"

Laugh. Cough. Laugh. Cough.

"I will wrestle you right now if you think I'm soft."

"I said wasn't…" Cough.

"Alright. Enough chatter. We have a long day tomorrow, and Truant needs his rest. That cough sounds heavy. Do you feel fever?"

"I don't know. Maybe a little."

"There's more root water in the tin if you wake during the night."

Truant's dreams are gripped by disease. Shadows, sweating, and a mind-bending "I'm sick" montage of delirium. Too many hooks in him for Zeke's powders to pry free, those hooks toss him and turn him until morn.

In the morning, Truant walks down into the middle tunnel to check his watch in the darkness. Still glowing like the night before. Cool. Before turning back to camp, he vomits root water and bile. Not cool.

His fever is worse. No need for the back of someone else's hand to tell him this, and now his stomach's in knots. It's official, gang, Truant's sick. Not sure how bad yet but either way, he and the Trates have to move on.

For several days they travel through the tunnel, sleeping and eating in cramped space. Deeper and deeper into ground, then back on a course towards the surface. The path never strays far to the left or to the right, though on several occasions it hooks large curves out and back in, following what might have once been an underground tributary. There are a few instances where the path curves so far in one direction that the glow in Truant's watch softens and the hands spin wildly, but when the path bows back towards their original direction, the watch brightens and the hands align, pointing the way. There are sections that require crawling or climbing. All the while, the watch glows.

Truant's condition perpetually worsens, passing between chills, fevers, and cold sweats that are a combination of both. The vomiting continues. His skin loses its color. Ezekiel gives him various herbs and powders each morning and night, but nothing stems the tide.

At night he tosses and turns and mumbles in his sleep. The mumbling genuinely disturbs Jake, who grows more distressed with his friend's situation by the minute. Through it all, Truant maintains his good humor and does his best to assure Jake everything's going to be okay, but there are other forces at play. Other forces an immune system isn't equipped to fight. The type of forces that bodies contend with on a metaphysical level. Emotions that breed cancers. Thoughts that feed those emotions. Demons that seed those thoughts. All that shit. Big Black Book shit.

3

"The path we took here, it can't be the normal way in or out for these people."

Our three travelers crouch behind a rock ledge on the shelf of a cliff, some fifty feet above the cave floor, peering at the sight below.

"What do you think we should do?" asks Truant, voice scratchy from days of persistent cough and vomit. He's badly congested now, a curdled wheeze to his speech.

"Watch."

Zeke retrieves his spyglass for a closer look at the encampment below. A tent city, really, in the largest cavern they've seen in the network of caves. Dwellings are scattered about, organized in small groupings throughout the space and at different levels of ground elevation. More permanent structures live in a central "valley" area where children play as the adults go about their business. A well-paced stream cuts the giant cavern in half. There's one large community fire pit and numerous small cooking pits in between circles of tents.

"If this is where they live, where do they go for food?" asks Jake.

"Good question. They either came in stored for a long haul, or we are near an exit to these caves. My guess would be the latter.

Have you seen any weapons?"

"No, but that doesn't mean there aren't any?"

"Good answer. One way or another we'll have to get past them, with or without their knowledge. They might be more put off if we're caught sneaking around their camp, or we could be taken against our will if we announce our presence. What do you think, son?"

"I think they have kids playing in the open. That means they feel safe but are probably ready to defend themselves too. If we show them we're here, they might capture us just to be careful."

"Agreed. I think the best course is to keep watching. They might show us an exit through their own normal movements, in which case we will wait until they bed for the evening and be on our way. Not dealing with them at all is my preferred choice. Truant, do you have any different thoughts?"

Truant doesn't answer. He hears Zeke's question, somewhere in the recesses of his foggy conscious self, which has now taken a backseat to his ill, delusional, barely still connected to reality cartoon self that is floating around the cave above him in an old-timey full-length nightgown and cap, teasing him to sleep, diving into a four-post bed with pillow in hand. He wants to tell Jake he's okay but he doesn't want to lie, and he's too feeble anyway, and that wasn't the question, was it? What was the question?

Is he awake or dreaming? Alive or dead? No, Zeke asked him something. That's the question. Isn't it? He's unsure, confused. The one thing he's certain of, deep down - I am a living creature who is connected to all things and therefore the universe itself - certain of, is that whatever's wrong with him isn't just making him physically sick. It's attacking his spirit and his braim. *"Brain, not braim. Brain, with an N."*

Our time jumper (and/or dimension hopper) nods his head yes to Zeke's question (it looks like that's what he's doing, at least) and then slumps to the side. Just before he passes out, Truant hears more words he's too foggy-headed to comprehend:

"I think he passed out."

And…

"There's no need to hide."

When Truant first wakes, he takes some time to remember where he is. Or, better yet, he takes some time to remember he doesn't know where he is. Wherever here is, he must be fairly safe. After all, he isn't tied down and someone has apparently nursed him back to health.

I was sick.

Sitting up on the cot. *This is a cot. I'm lying on a cot, in a tent.*

His eyes scan the inside of the tent as his braim digs in for a hefty recollection. Here we go. Memories creep forward like a slowly advancing tide running away from one large wave: His jaunt through the future.

I'm in the future.

Everything crashes in, from the moment he left Texas on foot to meeting Curtis Gout at the filling station to falling in with the Trates and all points in between.

Lift feet and turn. Whoa. Still groggy. Okay. Feet on floor. Up we go. Legs a little shaky, but I feel great. I do. I feel fantastic.

Stepping outside the medical tent he's been in for three weeks, Truant finds himself on a flat, elevated position. The cave floor slopes up into walls in all directions, with numerous little plateaus throughout, much like the elevated ridge he and the Trates had previously hidden behind, only this one not so high off the cave floor. Below and to his left, the gleeful chattering giggles of children beg for his attention.

The first time Truant sees the little prophet, the little prophet is spinning in circles with a bunch of other kids. Jake is with them. They spin until they fall, then stand and run, equilibrium in complete disarray, a master class in childish craft, PHDs in Laughing Wholeheartedly at One's Own Silliness on full display. If I've said it once, I've said it a thousand times over: Silliness is its own reward.

A few moments watching Jake revel in childhood then Truant scans for Zeke, who he quickly spots near Jake, as expected. Zeke sits off to the side writing in his journal and watching the children play.

"I suppose I owe you thanks."

"Well there you walk and talk. Welcome back to the living, Mr. Memphis. As for the thanks, you may only thank me for being ambushed. These people nursed you."

"How long was I out?"

"Three weeks."

"Three weeks? Holy cow."

"Yeah, I was beginning to think you weren't coming back, no matter what they told me. Nice mustache, by the way."

Confusion barnstorms Truant's face as the youngster reaches for his upper lip. Sure enough, there it is. He can feel it. The wispy, 'I'm not a man yet but I'm getting there,' whiskers of a teenage pencil-thin. "So, uh, what's been going on?" Not knowing where to begin with his questions, that one sort of falls out on its own as he continues poking at his upper lip.

"Not much really. You were infected with a demon, we've fallen in with a band of revolutionaries, and my son is playing games with a child prophet. Sound like fun?"

"That kid Jake was chasing…"

"That kid waiving at you."

Truant turns and sees the child holding hands with Jake, both excitedly waving hello with their free hand. He waves back and then returns his attention to Zeke, but before he can organize his thoughts to speak, arms wrap his waist from behind. Breaking the grasp, Truant turns and embraces Jake.

"Good to see you, buddy!"

"I knew you'd be okay! Frank said so. You can come meet him after."

"After what?"

"Frank says you need to talk to dad, then we can all play. So hurry up and get it over with and then I will introduce you to Frank!"

Before Truant can open his mouth to almost ask another question, Jake runs away, rejoining the other kids for another round of unadulterated child's play.

"Frank? Obviously I'm confused," says Truant, turning back to Zeke.

"Obviously. Shall we go for a walk? How are your legs? They exercised you while you were out, worked your arms and legs, but I bet they need stretching."

"Yeah, walking sounds good to me. Then some food maybe? I'm starving."

Zeke leads Truant in a different direction than the one from which they had discovered the encampment. They take a narrow tunnel east for a mile or so, then make a series of turns in all directions. Still discombobulated, Truant has no idea what direction they're facing when they come to a hidden opening. They pass through a man-sized crack in the cave wall that's concealed behind another rock formation. Almost anyone traversing this tunnel would walk past the hidden opening, assuming the formation is a solid part of the cave's wall and never squeezing behind it to find the passageway.

When they exit, Truant finds the opening on the other side equally well-concealed. Skirting around a fallen boulder encircled by several large stalagmites, they squeeze through another tunnel for several hundred yards before it opens into the outskirts of a real underground city. Not like the camp they've just left. This is an actual city. There are buildings built into the cave walls. Support structure has been installed throughout the giant cave to prevent collapse. Daylight shows through several large openings above the city, and something is generating electricity.

"Pretty impressive, huh?"

"To say the least."

"C'mon, we can trade for a snack."

"Wait. Zeke, why did you bring me here?"

"It's noisy down there. We can speak privately. And you said you were hungry."

As they walk into the city, Zeke catches Truant up to speed. The Weirdos, as Zeke playfully refers to them, had somehow known he, Jacob, and Truant were hiding up on the cliff.

"They found us right when you passed out. Would have been a tough go trying to fight our way out with you incapacitated. I didn't see much choice but to hope they were friendly. Luckily, they were."

"Thank you, Zeke."

"For what?"

"You could have left me."

"Oh. Hmph. I suppose I could have. Unfortunate. The thought never crossed my mind."

Not one to crack many jokes or smiles, the beleaguered upward crease in Zeke's mouth wasn't lost on Truant.

"I appreciate you, Zeke. And I'm glad they're friendly."

"Me too."

"So what happened after they found us? I mean, with me. Exactly."

"It was…" Zeke searches for the correct word, "…unusual. The boy said you weren't sick. He said you had been, 'infiltrated,' I believe was the word he used. Infiltrated. He whispered something in your ear, and then you exhaled, almost like a sigh, for a long time. It was very strange. I can't imagine you actually held that much air. Afterward, you did exactly what he said you would do next. You slept for three weeks without waking, to the day."

"Three weeks asleep? No food? No water?"

"They hooked a fluid bag, but no food and no waking up. I checked your breathing on several occasions to ensure you were still alive. Three weeks. Took the bag off this morning. Frank told 'em you wouldn't need it any more. You woke up a few hours later. I've never seen anything like it."

"And the kid's name is Frank?"

"Yes."

"Man, this is so weird."

"Exactly."

"I've never met a kid named Frank, you know. It's one of those names that only adults have, and you wonder, where do all these Franks come from when you never meet a kid named Frank."

"You're an odd young man, Mr. Memphis."

Both men fall silent as they enter the city, Zeke with purpose and Truant with wonder, as Zeke appears to be searching for a particular spot. There's a bazaar feel, vendors with booths and goods hanging from polls or tent canopies. A merging of well-maintained old-world technology, post-apocalyptic cinema-esque scrapping, and the neo-luminescent futuristic stylings of advanced cave-dwelling, whatever the hell that means. (I just write 'em, folks. These words don't always explain themselves to me either.)

"So, do you believe he's a prophet?"

"Let's not get into what I believe. I'm simply telling you what I witnessed. Hup, here we go." Zeke leads Truant to a food cart where he swaps a small cache of teas for two kabobs with chunks of meat and vegetables on them. "These are delicious," he says, handing one to Truant.

"What is it?"

"Best not to ask, I think. When you're hungry you eat."

"Ha. Fair enough."

Quick work is made of the kabobs as the two men walk and talk. "Apparently, there's a network of underground cities in this region, born from the natural cave system. The Weirdos' camp is intentionally hidden, hence the twist and turns in getting here. It took several attempts for me to memorize the path. They travel here for their supplies, and apparently remote communities in these caves are common, so no one questions when they come and go."

"Who runs the city?"

"I'm not sure, but it may be Frank."

"I don't understand. If he's in charge why would they hide? Why wouldn't they just stay here."

"To be safe, I think. Frank is the spiritual leader of a movement, and it appears they keep his location hidden as much as possible. From what I can tell, this city is loyal to him. Last week, I saw a small group come from here to meet with Frank and his caregivers. I think they were at the camp to receive orders. Or, perhaps, direction is more accurate."

"Jake said Frank told him that me and you needed to go talk. Do you think he can see the future? Do you think he knows what we're talking about?"

Silence, while Zeke searches for the correct response, his face a witch doctor's soup of countless imperceptible expressions. In another life, this exact same impossible-to-read but deeply internally emotive man would make a helluva gambler. Sorry, is a helluva gambler. That's another story for another day. One I most likely won't be allowed to tell.

"Truant, I've heard of these things before," Zeke finally says. "There have been rumors for years, rumors older than you, about a prophet or a leader or a movement that would come and change everything. Free the people. Save the world. This is human nature, I believe. Throughout history, we've sought and created saviors. It's the historical creed of the oppressed. Revolution is coming. The savior is coming. In recent years, talk like this has spread through lower Detroit. I can only assume other lower levels as well. People claiming a leader was, is out there, and the League of Cities is after them. I've never purchased in such talk. I thought it was nonsense."

"But you don't anymore?"

"Now it's more complicated. These are good people. They believe in that boy, but I don't believe in prophecy, Truant. Or magic. I don't."

"So how do you explain Frank?"

"I don't. I can't. No more than I can explain you being here." Zeke stops and turns to face Truant, near eye to eye. "I think you've grown."

"Well, they say you grow in your sleep."

"Do they?"

"C'mon, Zeke. You didn't answer my question about Frank before. You're dodging again. You said you brought me here to speak privately. Please, speak freely. I won't tell anyone."

Zeke's nostrils flare, a long, deep breath of oxygen and acceptance, patiently circulated through the body and exhaled with earnest trepidation. "I've led myself astray. This conversation, it's not what I intended."

"Then what did you intend? What did you want to tell me that you don't want the others to hear?"

"I'm not interested in wars or revolutions, Truant. Jake and I will leave this place. Continue our journey. I haven't told Jake, nor mentioned this to any of our new friends."

"Why?"

"They're believers. I don't want them trying to convince me to stay, or using Jake to do so, and he surely would, with or without their influence. And, if they believe they're protecting a prophet, they may try to hold us against our will, for fear we could expose them. Best to go without warning, and without a chance for Jake to argue."

"When will you leave?"

"As soon as you are ready if you intend to go with us. If not, then I wanted an opportunity to explain this to you. Say goodbye, before Jake and I disappear. Perhaps you could prepare a note for him."

"Zeke, you sound like you already know I'm not coming with you?"

"Nothing is certain, that's why we're having this conversation, but you're going to have some thinking to do and I ask that you do it quickly. In the end, I fear our paths will not continue together."

"Why? Why would you say that?"

"Because when the Weirdos found us, they said they were waiting for you."

When Ezekiel and Truant return to the encampment, Jake is anxiously waiting for them.

"Isn't the city awesome?"

"Yeah, it's pretty cool."

"We were really worried about you, but Frank said you would be okay and you are. Frank knows all kinds of stuff."

"That's what your dad said."

"Did he tell you that Frank knew you came from the past?" Jake whispers conspicuously, as a child enthralled in cosmic gobbledygoo rightfully should do.

"No."

"Well he did. He told me. Did my dad tell you that everyone here thinks Frank is some kind of, what was the word?"

"Prophet?"

"Prophet. Yeah. I'm not sure what that is, but I am pretty sure my dad doesn't think Frank is one, and I don't know if I do since I don't know what one is supposed to be. I know Frank sees the future. Even dad hasn't argued about that with what happened to you, but I don't know if that makes Frank a…prophet, but I really like Frank, and I think you will too."

"You been drinking coffee?"

"What? Oh. Very funny. I guess next time I won't be so happy you're alive."

"Ha. Let's hope there isn't a next time."

At dinner, Truant eats until his belly bloats and his jaw is sore from chewing. Then he meets Frank. The child prophet taps his right shoulder from behind, quickly dodging left when Truant turns to look. You remember that trick?

Truant turns back to look over his left shoulder, where Frank stands with a blissful smile.

"I'm Frank."

"Hi, Frank. I'm Truant."

"I know."

"Of course."

"Would you like to play games with us after dinner?"

"As long as I don't have to run around. I might puke." Truant pats his swollen belly with defeat.

"We'll play zombie tag," says Frank. "You can be first zombie."

"Zombie tag? I've never heard of that. Sounds like fun."

"It's more fun than meet the demon."

The prophet's face is solemn stone but Jake, who is sitting next to Truant, giggles half-chewed food from his mouth. A recurring habit for the boy. Truant glances at Jake, succumbing to his friend's infectious laughter, then rotates back to Frank. Frank simply smiles and runs away laughing.

To describe Frank requires a flexible understanding of perception. If I tell you he is a handsome child, you must accept that he may be something…else (I hesitate to label any child ugly to the public. Only among friends.). Ethnically, Frank somehow looks like he could belong to any culture. His skin tone, his bone structure, his eyes, his hair, they're unique and unoriginal at the same time. Furthermore, on a given occasion you might swear his hair is blond, other times damn near black, then later convince yourself it is somewhere in between, and the rest of his features go the same way.

While others may notice this phenomenon, it is never discussed. I think, perhaps, that Frank's presence frees the mind and heart of trivialities. Whether others notice or not, Truant does, swearing to himself that the child's features change, that somehow Frank manages to acclimate himself physically to whomever he's around, to make the other person more comfortable. If Frank met a leper, Truant would expect to see the boy suddenly peeling off skin.

The truth, as I see it now, is that Frank makes people more comfortable not because he changes, but because people see in him what they want to. What they need. Frankly (teehee), I'm not even certain Frank is a boy. I am defiantly certain it does not matter.

After dinner, the children play. Truant, physically closer to man than child, towers over the screaming little ones that he slow chases like a good zombie should. As the last spastic exaltations of youthful energy quiet and resistant children heed the tractor-beam of their parents' bedtime summons, Frank asks Truant to take a walk with him.

"The Trates told you about me, what everyone says about me, didn't they?"

"Of course they did. And I should thank you. Thank you for saving me, Frank."

"You're welcome, but I'll tell you a secret. I didn't really do anything." A few moments of silence and confusion from Truant, so Frank says, "I promise it will make sense later."

"How about you promise to explain it better later?"

"Maybe."

Truant decides this is an appropriate time for a playful nudge, then says, "Zeke said you were waiting for me. How did you know I was coming?"

"I said I was waiting for all of you. I like Mr. Trate, but I'm not sure he likes me."

"Oh, I'm sure he likes you, Frank. He just doesn't know what's going on. Neither do I for that matter. What is going on, Frank?"

"It's scary. Most of the time, I just want to be like the other kids, but I don't get to."

"I don't think that has to be true, Frank. You can be who you want to be. It's your life. Don't let people make you be something you don't want to."

"But it's not my life. I know that. And it's no one's fault. I have to be what I am."

"What are you, Frank?"

"I'm the prophet, silly."

"But how do you know that for sure?"

"Hold my hand. I'll show you."

Truant takes Frank's hand without hesitation.

"Now, close your eyes and don't be scared."

Don't be scared?

Classic.

To be fair, Frank is a child, despite being some sort of cosmic membrane through which universal knowledge and power are diffused, and children rarely understand their own tropey blunders.

Close your eyes and don't be scared? Hardy har, Frank. Has there ever been a more useless utterance than "don't be scared?" I mean, half the time if you say that it's because the other person is already in that state. The other half of the time, you just gave an unwitting participant reason to believe there is a reason they might oughta, indeed, be scared. Anyway…

Despite his immediate wondering whether or not there is a reason to suddenly be afraid, Truant closes his eyes. Frank closes his own, then gives Truant's hand a gentle squeeze before unleashing an almost stereotypical montage of images and emotions depicting universal knowledge as seen and read in the late twentieth and early twenty-first century science fiction zeitgeist, before honing in on the personal history of our time-wandering protagonist, both of which you may be familiar with, but I promise you Frank has absolutely zero notion of until now.

The image bombardment happens so fast it's hard for Truant to keep up, as time loses relevance in the order to which all things universal and personal are displayed. There's the birth of the universe, the Earth, and the history of man. Truant sees his family, before and after the car crash. Then outer space, and wars, and aliens. There's Heaven and Hell or at least something like what Truant thinks they might look like if they are real, or perhaps the very real versions of these places that humanity has concocted fantastical versions of. There're the Trates on the run and Curtis Gout spitting tobacco juice into the rain. There's Truant sick and Frank whispering in his ear. And the girl, that same one from the boat and the barn (y'all don't know about the barn yet, but that's another story for another day). Cities burn and fall into oceans and dinosaurs fly rocket ships. He sees other galaxies and planets and their histories, and people that live on those planets that look like him. He sees alternate dimensions side by side, splintering in infinite directions into infinite dimensions. He sees dogs driving trucks and wizards baking cakes and sentient moons standing guard over their planets. It's all very confusing, understandably, and of course Truant can't stop watching, nor make sense of it, but he squeezes Frank's hand tightly, refusing to let go.

More. More. Who would want this to end? Perhaps you, or me, but not this Truant. His nature defines his response. More. "Keep…giving…me…more," the unnecessary decree of the insatiable adventurer or drug addict, adventure perhaps simply being a healthier than average drug.

Finally, in a moment of vision-induced serenity, one I am not authorized to describe, Frank wrests his hand free of Truant's grasp. Truant, noticing the blood-flushed mark of his grip on Frank's hand and wrist, jolts back to reality.

"I'm sorry, Frank! I hope I didn't hurt you. I didn't know what I was doing."

"It's okay," says Frank, rubbing his hand. "I asked you to look. Sometimes people don't want to let go."

"What was all of that?"

"I think you know, don't you? Some of that stuff gets mixed up with my imagination, I think. I can't help it, but you get the idea, right?"

Truant nods his head.

"You want to hear something gross?"

"What?"

"If I try, I can see me being born."

"That's disgusting, Frank."

"I told you so," Frank says, then he starts laughing and Truant joins him, easing his general confusion for the situation. "Truant, someone made us special. Me and you, and the Trates. Someone or something decides who has to help take care of other people and the world and even outer space. They talk to me when they need to, and tell me what to do."

"What do they sound like?"

"It's not like that. I don't actually hear them, they just put thoughts in my head?"

"Who do you think they are?"

"They are everything and everywhere. They are everyone at the same time and everyone by themselves."

The questions fall silent as Truant ponders the concept of universal knowledge and the interconnectivity of all living things, while Frank notices an interesting rock. Frank retrieves it, dusting it off and slipping it into a pocket, leaving Truant to his thoughts. With short time more questions come.

"If you don't think Zeke believes you, why didn't you show him, the way you just showed me?"

"I offered. Mr. Trate declined, and I don't like to force people to see."

"I guess that's not a surprise. So why were you waiting for us?"

"Because I knew you were coming, and we are all supposed to be together for a while."

"That's not exactly what I mean."

"I understand, but it's hard to know how much to tell, especially when everyone wants you to tell them everything. And I don't always see everything. A lot of the time I only get pieces."

"That seems counterproductive."

"What's that?"

"I'm just saying, whoever is in charge or whatever, and made you this way, it seems like they could just do a better job telling you what they want."

"I think maybe if they did, it might still be hard for me to tell other people everything."

"Well, you can tell me whatever you want on your own time, when you feel like it, how's that?"

"Thank you."

"Hey, here's a question that is probably okay to answer. How old are you, really?"

"I think I'm ten. No one knows for sure."

"Where are your parents?"

"The same place as yours," Frank says, and then he kicks Truant in the shin.

"Ow! Ha ha. What did you do that for?"

"I didn't want you to feel sad for me," Frank says. Then he plugs his thumbs in his ears and sticks his tongue out of his mouth, and waggles his fingers, taunting his new friend, and Truant chases him all the way back to camp.

"Why did you say he was waiting for me, Zeke? Frank said he was waiting for all of us." Truant sits with Zeke outside the tent they were given by Frank's people. An appreciated show of hospitality, though none of them use it for sleeping. Zeke prefers to sleep outside and Jake, currently snoring magnanimously, prefers to do whatever his father does. Truant just doesn't care for tents in general. They always smell funny.

"Each of us has his own life to live," Zeke replies. "His own 'part to play.' I wanted to afford you the opportunity to consider yours without feeling tied to Jake and I, or the way I feel. Our course is set. Whether Frank thinks he was waiting for Jake and I or not, he was not. If he was waiting for 'us,' it is because we were with you."

"Well then, what if I asked you to stay?"

"Please don't. I want land and fresh air, and to raise my son somewhere decent. If there is someone or something out there running this show, then I ask who or whatever it is to respect my wishes and leave us the hell alone."

"I'm not sure life works that way," says Truant.

"Me neither. But my feet and my compass surely do."

Night. Dreams. Truant's first slumbering fantasies in weeks with the coma and whatnot. Who knows what boiled in the ol' brain stew while the demon had grips on him? Maybe he dreamed. Maybe he and the demon played hippocampus chess. Maybe he was simply at peace.

By the way, the demon's name is Scurry. Scur for short. I'm not sure how Scur got in the eel that bit Truant, or if that's how it got in Truant at all. I'm not sure where Scur went next after leaving Truant. What I do know is Scur has a cousin demon named Zorn, who I will meet when I'm much older than in this adventure, (another story, another day, etcetera etcetera, yada yada).

The dream. Back to the dream. Truant's piloting a spaceship with Jake as his co-pilot. Zeke is the gunner, and they're in a dogfight with other spaceships. The other ships don't have pilots. They're all suspended from strings that go nowhere, with some invisible puppeteer puppeteering away. The enemy ships fly in formation and Truant flies circles around them while Zeke picks them off one by one, but they just keep reappearing. Eventually, all the enemy ships break formation. They reform, hovering in a pattern shaped like a word: EVIL. After the word is formed, Zeke fires a single shot that hits the center of the pattern and the whole thing explodes, at which time the dream merges with scenes from the victory celebration in the original *Star Wars*. The *original* original, without any of the stupid computer graphics.

Star Wars was the last movie Truant watched with his family before his parents and sister were killed. I don't think it was a new release at the time. Anyway, I'm convinced that dreams rarely have meaning for our real lives. In my present opinion, dreams are purely a reflection of your brain trying to cope with and organize all the madness we're confronted with when awake. Nothing more or less. Assigning excessive value to dreams is the folly of trusting an untestable scientific hypothesis because you can't form a comprehensive core testing group when you can't remember them all. Of course, I say this to you as I sip bourbon in the future while telling you a story about my past that occurred in a further future because "time travel" (or…maybe it's just dimension hopping…?).

So, what do I know? Maybe dreams are real.

Return from coma, day two. After breakfast, Frank takes Truant on another walk. Now they sit alone together, once again.

"Did you know that you were born to be a hero?"

"I'm sorry?"

"It's true," says Frank. "You're a hero. You're going to help save the universe?"

Who wouldn't want to hear that nonsense? Right? Truant chuckles, uncomfortable with the notion, and says, "How about we just start with the world?"

Frank returns laughter fire, then says, "I'm serious. Why do you think you found the portal?"

"You know about the portal?"

"Of course."

"I guess I should have figured that."

"I'm sure you would have, if the thought had crossed your mind."

A little side-eye here, from teenager to tiny prophet. Playful, to be sure, but extremely well done.

"I wasn't sure how to tell you before," says Frank. "But last night I had a dream and I learned how."

(What was that I recently said about dreams, again?)

"Well then out with it, goofball, before I put the world's smallest prophet in a camel clutch?"

"What's the camel clutch?"

"I'll teach you about the Iron Sheik later. Now come on, out with it."

"What's an Iron Sheik?"

"Out with it."

"Okay, okay. It's hard. Sometimes I feel like I know all this stuff but I don't understand any of it. I have answers but I don't know what questions they are for. Does that make sense?" Frank's look of honest confusion surprises Truant.

"Wait until you're a teenager," Truant says. "I feel all kinds of questions inside of me, but I can't put the words together to ask most of them."

Frank's confusion switches to…nervousness? Trepidation? Something along those lines if I'm reading a child prophet correctly. "I'm not sure I get to be a teenager."

(You saw that coming, right?)

Frank stares for at least a few miles, if not a thousand, then glances at the hand Truant places on his shoulder and smiles, face changing from child to ageless sage and back again. "So, last night in my dream I asked the voice for help, and this is what it told me to tell you. Are you ready?"

"Yes."

"This will be like what I showed you before, but different. Sometimes it scares people, so don't be scared."

"Okay." (Again with the "Don't be scared" nonsense!)

"Close your eyes and hold my hands," Frank says. "If my voice sounds different, it's because I'm not really talking. I'll be inside your head."

"Okay."

"Are you ready?"

"Yes."

"Hear what I hear."

And he does. The Voice of All Voices. Countless wise tones. The aged turtle. The owl. The burning bush. The tree. The kung-fu Sifu. The disembodied boom of the cosmos. The dulcet tone of all mother planets. The moons that move the tides and on and on. All spoken and heard at once, creamily oozing from one voice to the other, word by word, into one mesmerizing, hypnotic, commanding, loving revealer of secrets. The Voice of All Voices.

"I am here, 'other' to this earthly child. Always present, silent or no. You hear me, Truant. Yes, you hear. Hear this: All are bound. One organism. One, infinite existence. One.

Perception of the forces that unite all living things is limited by sentience. Limited by the very notion of life and death. Do you see?

The fullness of existence is beyond the comprehension of mortal ego. Beyond the comprehension of physical sentience. Existence is boundless, ruled by chaos and order at once. Every possible possibility must be, including no possibilities at all. Do you see infinity?"

"No."

"Correct. And you cannot see the eternal conflict existence suffers. A conflict between the fundamental forces that may define existence or destroy it. A conflict whose battles fall to the shoulders of those most insignificant yet significant. Like the cells of your physical structure. Innumerable. Replaceable. Yet each one the divine spark of life. You were chosen before you were ever born."

"I don't understand."

"You never will. This was a die cast at the beginning of the game when life insisted upon itself and sprang forth. Everyone plays a role. Some more than others. Our souls are the soldiers. You were chosen to help save this universe. That is why you found the portal, and why you found me."

"How? How am I supposed to help save the world?"

"Not the world, Truant. Your world is a tiny piece of a much larger puzzle. An atom, in a body infinite. This entire universe, and therefore everything else that is, depends on you, if only for a moment. As for how, I cannot answer."

Why? Truant thinks, with more thoughts quickly following in frustrated verse, stealing the unnecessary words from his mouth and these pages.

"I know not," replies the Voice, hearing Truant's unspoken question. "I know what I'm told, the same as you and this child when I speak to it. Many came before you bearing the same burden, and many will follow. You are not alone, you never will be, and despite the seriousness of this burden, you can't take life too seriously. We are all but a blip. Even this Voice created by the ages."

"How can I do something if I don't know what I am supposed to do? What if I fail? How will I even know if I've failed? And how in the world am I not supposed to take all of this too seriously?"

"Because you were born with a light heart and playful spirit. Both of which, the terror of life may strip from you. Especially when you see and feel all the pain. The only way you will fail is by not being true to your nature. You've been set to win by the greatest of all powers. The forces against you will only defeat you with your help. Take heed, this is a crucial moment in our existence, but may not matter at all. Do you see?"

"No."

"Good. You never will. Not when presumption destroys possibility. Infinity by nature includes silliness, Truant. And absurdity.

Both the playful and painful. The painful: Life is out of balance. On the verge of an oblivion. Evil forces have tipped the present scale and billions of people, trillions of creatures you will never see or even know exist, are counting on you. The playful: You might save them all with something so simple as the joy felt while playing a child's game. And no sooner than our part is done, it will be someone else's turn. Take comfort in who you are and do not lose sight of your nature, because none of this may matter, but it might mean everything."

"I don't understand. What's the point of all of this if it might not matter?"

"Life. That's it. That's the point. Life happens and happens and happens. The infinite measure of life, and all that infinity may be."

Frank lets go of Truant's hands and they both open their eyes. Frank looks tired. Like he's ready for a nap. Then his expression changes and the lights in his eyes return.

"Race you back to camp," Frank says, standing and shaking his hips to taunt his new friend.

"You better start running!"

They race back to camp, laughing. Later, Truant will marvel over how quickly he let go of everything the Voice told him and started having fun again. Being in the presence of Frank is great for that.

Late the same evening, Jake has fallen asleep. Time for a private conversation with Ezekiel.

"Zeke, now that Jake's out, I'd like to tell you something. Something you probably won't agree with."

Zeke marks the page of his journal and sets the weathered

notebook aside. "You may speak your mind with me. I hope you already feel that comfort."

"I do. I do. I guess I'm just kind of preparing you because you asked me not to ask, so I won't. I'm not gonna ask, but I will tell you, I think you and Jake should stay with Frank." Truant musters as much of his perception of manly confidence as he can when he speaks that last part. The drop in vocal tone is not lost on Zeke.

"I had a feeling this subject was not at rest. I suppose you have your own argument to support the one my son has been pressing me with?"

"Is Jake giving you a hard time? I'm sorry if I helped cause that."

"The two of you are not in cahoots?"

"No. Not at all. I promise. That would be disrespectful of you, Zeke. I know how you feel. Jake has talked to me about what he wants, but I wouldn't lead a son against a father. Not a good father, at least." Scarlett hues flush Truant's cheeks with the realization of the words that just escaped him. Who the hell is he, a teenager, to report on Zeke's work as a father?

Of course, Zeke, being the man that Truant perceives him to be, properly receives the compliment. "Thank you, Truant. I appreciate your words and your respect. That's an admirable quality in you, among many I've witnessed. If I'm given license to judge, I suspect you will make a fine father someday. Now, as for staying with Frank, it is too late for you to impose your will upon me. We are leaving tomorrow." Zeke watches Truant's face sink, with a sudden tinge of guilt for his maneuvering. "I hope you will be going with us."

"I want to Zeke, but I don't think I'm going to be able to."

"That's a shame. Frank and Jake will both be disappointed."

"What?"

"The whole camp leaves tomorrow and heads south. Jake and I will travel with the young prophet and his people for as long as they move in our common direction. Will you join us?"

Sucking wind through clenched teeth, Truant weighs the decision with mock consideration and says, "I don't know, Zeke. I was just kind of getting used to these caves."

Zeke smiles wide, a rare-ish phenomenon if you haven't been keeping track.

"I thought you didn't want any part of a revolution. What changed your mind?"

"You," says Zeke. "And Frank. Apparently, what Frank and I both seek is not so far apart. Certainly much closer than I imagined."

"Well, you're gonna have to tell me more than just that."

"What Frank sees as his purpose and what other people seem to want from him are two very different things. I can only assume that Frank is the one in the right. True, some of his followers want a revolution. They believe Frank will somehow bless them with victory if they go to war. But what Frank wants, as he has explained to me, is a movement. A revolution of the mind and spirit. Not an armed conflict. Frank wants to show people how to live happily in a cruel world. How to save their own souls. Oppression only works when accepted."

Surprise. I would say that's the expression on Truant's face. Perhaps surprise mixed with ever-growing appreciation.

"You're not the only one Frank's had his conversations with," Zeke says. "He and I have spoken alone on many occasions. He's very convincing."

"Yes he is." (Even then at my young age, I should have known Frank would convince Zeke to stay.)

"Frank's interest, it seems, is setting an example. Showing people a way, rather than leading an army. His followers with a different agenda…Frank will eventually find himself at odds with them.

He knows this too." Zeke lights two smokes and tosses one to Truant. "And the League of Cities is after him. They know he exists, and they don't know what he is, so they are afraid of him. As his following grows, eventually they will track him down. That appears inevitable. In the end, I think Frank may find himself looking for the same thing as Jake and I."

Camp folds the next day and the gathering leaves. They move southwest through the caves for many days, underneath the marsh-covered lands of Kentucky until they reach the southern border, where the caravan turns southeast after crossing into the caves of Tennessee. The underground system is a marvel, with manmade expansion connecting multi-regional cave systems.

Our trio becomes a foursome, then a fivesome. Although Frank is diligent in sharing himself with all his followers, he chooses his new friends as bunkmates. Frank's tent is always set next to Truant's and the Trates'. The father and son pistoleers' inclination for sleeping outside naturally facilitates their transition to guardsmen.

A woman named Pete (short for Petunia) and a man named Dale, though not a romantic couple, act as Frank's surrogate parents and closest advisors. Pete is reserved, though her presence and emotional resonance often speak volumes without care for words. She's attractive, not lost on Zeke, and carries herself in a soothing, motherly way defined by strength. There is a perpetual sadness within her, Truant has surmised, because whenever Frank makes her smile there's always something else in her eyes. Something that states Frank has only softened a deep, burdensome pain. Truant is also pretty sure that Pete has noticed that Zeke has noticed, know what I mean?

Dale is a different story. Dale makes Truant uneasy. There's darkness around Dale. Just a feeling, but Truant doesn't trust him or his intentions toward Frank. Presumption lumps Dale in as one of the followers Zeke is suspicious of, wanting Frank to lead people to war, but Truant never mentions this to Zeke and certainly not Frank. Whatever Truant's own concerns, Frank proves time and again to be one step ahead of them all, and where others who suffer irrational needs for control might find this uncomfortable, Frank's prescience gives Truant peace.

As they travel, serious conversations about gods and universes and revolutions are rare, allowing the notion of any supposed hero responsibilities to slip from Truant's worries. Instead, the travelers enjoy their journey, treating rationed meals like feasts, playing games, and singing around their fires in the evenings. Frank develops into a relentless tease, likely a reflection of Jake's feisty presence and Truant's natural inclination for big-brothering. Yet, the little prophet also moves through camp every morning giving hugs, asking his followers how their previous day was and how they feel.

A joy filled journey, until it isn't. "Nothing lasts forever," they say, but I blame that on whoever said that crap first. Whoever unleashed this truth on our language, when it could have simply gone unspoken. Screw that dude or dudette.

What am I talking about? Segues, baby. Segues.

The fun always has to come to an end, right? Stupid "yin and yang, cosmic balance, can't have nothin' good ever last" universe we live in. It happens around the fire, after dinner and before bed. You know, the absolute best time to drop some shit on someone: Right before sleep.

Frank surprises Truant, and not in a good way. Truant, Zeke, Jake, Frank, and Pete all sit together. Dale is off doing whatever he does while the rest of them relax and enjoy each other's company. Frank surprises them all, except maybe Pete.

"I have to tell you something that makes me sad," Frank says, right out of the rhetorical metaphorical blue. Ears prick and residual chatter stops. "We don't get to stay together much longer. I don't want you to be sad, but it's true and I have to tell you."

"Are you sure?" Zeke asks.

"Yes, I'm sorry but I don't think we have much time left."

"Of course you're sure," Zeke mumbles.

"Who's leaving Frank?" asks Jake. "Who's going where? What's gonna happen to us?"

"I don't know Jakey. I can't tell. I'm sorry."

This is the first time Frank has appeared unhappy since Truant met him. Pete welcomes Frank onto her lap, holding him tight and humming gently to him.

"Frank," says Truant, "why did you tell us?"

"Because I know, and it's not fair, and I thought maybe we should say something to each other, while we still can."

"Not fair to who?" Truant asks.

"Like what?" Jake asks. "What are we supposed to say?"

Frank's answer is quiet compassion. Empathy. First, responding to Truant. Eyes meet, Frank's stating that he understands Truant's frustration and that yes, Frank may have indeed had a moment of weakness where he didn't want to carry the burden of knowing by himself. Truant looks away, softened, using a stick to aimlessly scratch at the cave floor dirt of an unforgiving universe as Frank persists in his silent exchange with the rest of his inner circle, Jake the last, with Frank imploring the young gunfighter to find answers to his questions within.

One by one, each head bows the acceptance of truth, a

deafening silence in respect of whatever may come next, until Truant breaks the accord.

"Like I love you, Jake," Truant says. A brief glance at Frank, who nods approval, then Truant returns his attention to Jake. "This is a time for saying things like that. I was born with brothers and a sister, Jake, but you're my brother now too. I love you as much as any of them. And I love you too, Zeke, whether you like it or not."

"This is mutual, my friend," Zeke says.

"I love you too, Truant. You and dad and Frank are my best friends. You too Pete, even though you don't ever talk." Jake's quip brings them all to laughter. Some tears.

Frank loosens from Pete's grip and gives everyone long hugs, encouraging them to do the same with each other. Truant slugs Jake in the arm when he notices Pete and Zeke holding each other a little longer than required, and Jake slugs Frank who is already watching, and Frank slugs Truant just because, and all three laugh when Pete and Zeke realize they're being watched, before coughing and throat-clearing their way out of the moment. Zeke turns a playfully threatening scowl on the boys. Pete blushes and smiles. The boys all laugh even harder.

Remember that sound, Truant. Remember that sound.

The next morning a large, camp-wide breakfast is prepared. Frank scurries about, saying good morning to everyone, hugging the adults and teasing the other children. Truant watches, especially reflective after the previous evening's conversation. Of course he wonders who might be leaving. And why. Initially, Truant might have assumed Jake and Zeke would depart, but Zeke gave his word to Frank. Unless something unavoidable happens, releasing Zeke against his will from his commitment to Frank, the only other logical option is Truant. Had Frank really been warning him? Preparing him for separation?

Our teenage time traveler (or probably actually more likely a dimension hopper but you get the point) attempts to let his worries slip away, but they won't, and the conversation he had weeks earlier with Frank plays on loop in his mind. *I don't want to be a hero*, he thinks, but somewhere inside, every child wants to be a hero. Or a villain. Truant simply doesn't want to pay the price, if that price means being separated from this new family. Traveling with Jake, Frank, Zeke, and Pete feels right. He doesn't want that to change, and the whole damn deal is making his stomach hurt. Stomachs are often the first to know when change is coming.

Breakfast ends and the little community is breaking camp when the change locomotive comes barreling down its inevitable tracks. From seemingly out of nowhere an announcement booms through the camp.

"Attention! You are being detained by the Coalition Security Forces of the League of Cities. Your camp is surrounded. Anyone who fails to comply with our orders will be shot on sight under the authority of League Chairman, Devlin Primm. Do not move. Everyone lay face down on the ground with their hands over their heads. Your camp will be searched. I repeat, do not move!"

At this, everyone in the camp immediately scatters into chaos. The CSF opens fire, as additional soldiers come out of hiding and move in.

"Come, everyone!" Dale screams, as he picks Frank up and flees.

"Everybody move," Zeke shouts, grips already in hands, rounds booming forth.

Everyone takes flight. Dale is in the lead, carrying Frank, who eventually wiggles his way free and runs on his own. Jake is next to them firing away, clearing a path with Pete and Truant right behind and Zeke in the back unloading his guns. They duck into a tunnel that leads West, the wrong direction.

Opening fire was a mistake on Zeke's part. The CSF didn't known who they were looking for. When the Trates began shooting it gave the soldiers a target on which to focus.

Despite their lack of firearms, Frank's people aren't pushovers. A few have various weapons, and many of them fight bravely with bare hands and grit. They occupy a glut of soldiers, though a healthy number still trail our hero and his friends.

Racing through the tunnel, Truant's group is in the lead followed by a group of soldiers followed by a group of Frank's people. The chase lasts for at least ten minutes until they reach a large open cavern. Around fifty feet across and one hundred feet long, the cavern is populated with fallen rocks and shelves to provide cover. A group of six, the Trates, Truant, Frank, Pete, and Dale all take shelter behind a large patch of stalagmites.

Soldiers flood through the opening of the cavern as Jake and Zeke pump the "hammers" on their guns. Zeke has succumbed to a fit of giggles, laughing and screaming at the enemy, but Truant is fixated on Jake, who throws him a wink and then rises stoically from behind his cover, firing at the enemy. Jake's demeanor is the exact opposite of his father's. He works his pistols with a calm sternness and severity that genuinely frightens Truant.

"Don't kill!" says Frank. "Please, please, no killing for me! No matter what!"

"Don't worry, kid," says Zeke. "Anybody dies by my hand it's on my soul."

"Please!"

"It's okay, Frank," says Jake, calmly. Almost robotically. No, hypnotically? Almost. Maturely. That's it. Maturely. This is adult Jake speaking. "I'm a dead shot for legs and arms and so's my father." To be clear, it's not the guns that are briefly morphing Jake into the man he'll someday become. It's not the goddamn guns.

Frank's people flood through the entrance, ambushing the soldiers. Many fire guns taken from fallen soldiers. Others hurl rocks or simply rush the men, overpowering them with group numbers. Bullets and charges of energy like Truant has never seen before are flying in all directions when Frank grabs Truant's hand and pulls him away.

"Come with me!"

"Frank," Pete cries.

"No! Come back!" Dale shouts, but it's too late. Frank and Truant scurry through the room, ducking behind rocks and under gunshots.

"Wait, what are you doing?" Truant begs. "My backpack!"

"Leave it. It's time to go!"

"But I need it!" Truant pleads, as Frank tugs him into another tunnel off the side of the cavern.

"Jake, follow them!" Zeke shouts.

Under the cover of fire from his father, Jake bolts through the room and into the tunnel that Truant and Frank entered.

"Where are we going?" Truant begs. "We shouldn't leave the others!"

"Look," Frank says, pointing at Truant's wrist. Truant's watch is glowing again, but brighter than before. This time it glares as brightly as it had when Truant stood in front of the portal that brought him to the future.

Oh no, thinks Truant.

"Wait!" Jake races after the two from behind, carrying Truant's backpack. Frank leads Truant into a passage on the right. Most would have run past the opening without even noticing.

There it is.

"In here, Jake!" Frank yells.

Jake runs into the little room and stops dead in awe. There before him are Frank, Truant, and some sort of weird, floating, shimmering light.

"What are you guys doing?" Jake huffs, trying to catch his breath.

"It's time for Truant to go, Jake."

"But I don't want to, Frank. Not yet, not now, you guys…"

"I know, but it's time. I don't want you to go either. But you have to. You have a job to do."

"What is that thing?"

"It's how I got here, Jake, only I don't know how it got here. Frank, how did you know this was here?"

"I didn't until we were here. I told you before, I don't always know what's happening or how to explain it. This stuff just…comes through me? I don't know the best way to say it."

"Then how do we know this is the right one? How do we know it will take me where I'm supposed to go?" The desperation in Truant's voice betrays not only his desire to stay but also his acceptance that he knows he must go, whether he wants to or not.

"Because this is the one, and that's what they do. They take you where you're supposed to be. You know you have to go, Truant. You have to." Frank doesn't say it aloud, but the tear running away from his left eye screams, *I don't want you to go either!*

"But I didn't even get a chance to say goodbye." This is a whimper, a cry for help from the forever child we all subconsciously cling to.

"Yes, you did. Last night. Now take this with you and go." Franks reaches into a pocket and pulls out a rusty skeleton key, placing it in Truant's hand.

"I can't leave. How do I know you'll be safe?"

"You must and you don't. You have to go, or it won't matter if we're safe or not."

There's a beat here where Truant looks at the skeleton key and then clenches his fist tightly, as tightly as he can.

"You knew. You knew and you didn't tell me."

"I did tell you. I told everyone."

"But I don't understand! What was the point of all this if I'm just leaving you now?! What was the point of any of this!?" Water fills Truant's eyes, bubbling forth from the deepest of wells.

"I told you before. Life is the point. This is your life. You're alive and this is part of your journey. You get to take all of this with you."

Truant shakes his head in frustration, then grabs Jake and hugs him tight. "Tell your dad I said goodbye."

"I will, I promise."

"I'll miss you, Jake."

A shakier lip than Truant's has never cried goodbye. Until a second later, when Jake openly weeps and says, "I'll miss you too."

Truant releases Jake, runs the back of his arm across his eyes, and turns to Frank.

"What is this?" he asks, turning the old rusty key over in his hand.

"It's a key, silly. I found it before you came. You'll know when to use it."

"How will I know?"

"It's a funny shaped old key." Frank smiles. "You'll know."

"Will we ever all see each other again?" asks Jake.

"In our dreams, Jakey," replies Frank. "I'm sure we will all be together in our dreams."

Truant grabs Frank and smothers him into his chest, holding on for as long as he can, and Jake puts his arms around them both until shouts are heard from out in the tunnels. Frank gently pushes against Truant, who releases the little prophet, then turns toward the portal. He takes a step forward then stops abruptly.

"Frank, there's something I have to know. I don't know why I never thought, never asked before, but I have to know."

Footsteps and gunshots echo from the tunnel walls.

"What is it? Hurry. You've got to go."

"When I was sick before, Zeke said you whispered in my ear. What did you say? What did you whisper in my ear?"

"Oh, that." Frank replies with oddly timed cheerfulness. "I told the demon I loved him," he says, and then he shoves Truant into the portal.

THE END.

Elsewhere

"What the hell is that thing?"

Ezekial Trate, Jakob Trate, and a child prophet named Frank stand in front of a shimmering light that hovers several feet off the ground. Hearts pounding. Panting from their flight into this hidden cavern. These are not the men I knew.

Zeke has just asked the question most obvious.

"It's a doorway," answers Frank. "A portal of some form."

"To where?" asks Jake.

"I don't know."

"Do you think it's safe?"

"Irrelevant, son. We're not going in that thing."

"No, we're not," Frank agrees. "It's not meant for us."

"Not meant for us? How do you know that?"

"Because, Jake. I think I invented them."

Coming Soon

The Human Trates

At age 29, after a successful career as a field Agent during which he saved the Universe on at least 514 separate occasions, Truant Memphis was promoted to archives. Bored off his ass while cataloguing Universal knowledge, Truant secretly began filing his fictional stories, recollections, and half-truths as real life cannon. Your reality may be one of his stories. Don't worry. You're still real.

You're welcome.

www.truantmemphis.com

www.ingramcontent.com/pod-product-compliance
Lightning Source LLC
Chambersburg PA
CBHW060505300726

48975CB00008B/2650